Parable of Stones
&
Other Stories

Zdravka Evtimova

ISBN 13: 9780998071763

Library of Congress Control Number: 2017940137

Cover Photo: Mihaela Mihaylova, Bulgaria
Author Photo by Polish poet Ewa Zelenay

Cover design by All Things That Matter Press
Published in 2017 by All Things That Matter Press

Table of Contents

Parable of Stones

"Write this down and read it ten times a day. Men are stones, all of them, and there's no exception to this rule," she says. "It's up to you if you'll have him, a large millstone tied around your neck, so the only thing you can do is jump in the river and drown. Or, you can chuck him into the mud and step on him so your shoes won't get any dirt on them."

She's a middle-aged woman, and her fame has spread far and wide in Struma Valley, Bulgaria. If business is bad, or you are unlucky in love, sick at heart, or fed up to the back teeth with life in general, you ask her advice. She charges you ten Levs.

"I've made up my mind to leave my husband," I tell her. "I need to be away from him, but he's not a bad man."

"How come he's not a bad man? He's a rotten man," the woman thunders. "Walk out on him without delay. Guys are a dime a dozen, believe me, and each one of them is after your scalp. He skins you and goes and boasts to his buddies you've cried your heart out for him. He's not a bad guy, eh? Then why are you talking to me? What did you shell out ten Levs for?"

"I don't know."

"Listen to me now. I'll tell you a story and I hope you'll understand once and for all, there're no good-natured guys under the sun. They are rubble. If you're clever you'll throw your husband under the bus, or even better, you'll hurl him at another bloke's head. Listen now and don't interrupt me, girl."

She speaks softly as if I am not there.

"I was blazing like a torch, head over heels in love with a young guy, a petty trader that sold brandy in the town of Pernik. One day he came to my orchard and studied my plum trees, but I doubted he saw anything in particular. He wasn't paying attention to the fruit—you can take my word for it—he gave me the eye instead.

"You're very pretty," he said.

"Go spin yarns somewhere else," I spoke very openly to him. "We've many mirrors in our house."

"But you are! Why don't you believe me?"

"What do you want?" I asked. I knew what he was after. I possessed a whole slope, every square yard of it, planted with plum trees. You see, I was a wily thing and I still am. It's true I have freckles across my cheeks, but this doesn't mean I'm unable to do my job standing on my head.

I bought a long hill, then another one, so I held all plum trees in the district in my hands. The plums are a woman's best friend; you should not forget that, my dear girl. Plums are brandy in the future tense.

"You are very intelligent," the petty trader said.

"I am," I agreed. "If you're here to buy my plums, let's speak business. I don't have time for anything else."

"I want five hundred kilos of plums."

"How much are you ready to pay per kilo?"

"How much do you want?" he asked.

"I'll let you drink a glass of my plum brandy first," I said. "Just one glass and it's on me. Then you'll tell me how much you're willing to pay."

"Okay." In a flash, he downed the brandy I gave him, and his eyes gleamed eager to slit my throat.

"I noticed something," I pointed out. "You are a lousy drinker. I can see blood in your eyes and more blood on your hands. But I may be wrong. Haste makes waste, so come to my kitchen," I looked him in the face. "I'll try another method to test how much you are worth, mister. You must drink one more glass of my brandy. I become beautiful after the second glass."

"Even if I don't drink a drop, you look prettier to me than the chicks on TV," the guy said. "But I'm ready to drink four glasses for you."

"More brandy in your head will do you no good," I said as he drank the second glass."

"I'll be honest with you, my girl," the woman turns to me, her eyes fastening on my face, "Love happens after the second glass. No second glass and the guy constantly finds fault with you. It'll be your nose that might seem too long; your legs will be far from perfect, but after the second one your nose and legs are a treasure.

Well, the trader's love was nothing much to speak of. Quite a few blokes have drunk two glasses of my brandy, and a lady learns to judge a guy by the way he finishes his drink.

"The first glass of brandy shows you the fire pit over which he will roast you once he has you eating out of his hand. Men are wicked, my dear. The second glass tells you if he's got a heart of gold or a bottle of poison in his chest. The petty trader's heart was neither fish nor fowl. I was at a loss.

"Look here," he said. "I'll pay you as much as you want for half a ton of plums. I'll pay you as much as you want even if I don't buy the plums. The only thing I care about is to drink two more glasses of brandy with you."

"No way," I said. "I'll drive a hard bargain, mister, and I make no secret of this fact. Half a ton costs one thousand Levs, but I'll take two thousand from you because I don't like you. And this is to make you go home. Good buy."

"*No*. I don't want to go. I fell in love with you," he said. "Your brandy's strong. It gives me so much power that I can't make out if I walk on the clouds or along the street to my mom's place."

"Okay. Give me the money and you'll have the plums: two grand."

"I don't have that much."

"Then why are you wasting my time? You guzzled my brandy already."

"It's because I like you so much."

"Oh, come off it," I told him.

I took all his cash, that was all there was to it. I carefully searched his pockets, extracting every bill or coin I could lay my hands on. Any guy deserves that; fleece him, take his money and send him to another woman. Let her wash his socks and listen to the loads of baloney he'll be babbling day and night.

"I respect my husband," I mutter under my breath as I stare at the woman. "He's kind-hearted."

"Yes, he's kind-hearted as long as he doesn't meet a mademoiselle blonder than you, my dear. She'll grab his money, then they'll drink two glasses of brandy together, and you will iron his shirts. A day later, he'll say he's unhappy, and you're supposed to wipe off his tears for him.

Now listen to the end of my story, and you'll learn a thing or two.

"I won't go home," the petty trader repeated.

I tell you, my dear girl, the brandy we make in the town of Pernik is magnificent. After the second glass, the guy falls in love with you, and after his third, he'd die for you. But love happens only to living men, doesn't it? So, I collected the guy's pants, shirt, and jacket, rolled them into a ball, and tossed everything into the street.

"I'm not a hotel manager, and my house can't accommodate you. Goodbye," that was what I told the petty trader.

On the following day, the guy came to my shop again.

"You are very pretty," he stammered. "*You are.* Let's drink two more glasses."

"I've already sold the plums to another man," I informed him.

"Did he drink brandy with you?"

"Yes."

The petty trader burst into tears, his cheeks shone wet, his closed eyelids fluttered, and he was a sorry sight. I'd been selling plums for five years and many a time had I drunk two glasses of brandy with the most attractive buyers, but none of them had ever sobbed like this.

"You are a peach," the buyers said, but I didn't swallow the bait.

Remember, it's the brandy that's a peach, not you. You may apply a truckload of makeup on your face or spread a layer of *fond de teint* a foot deep over your pores. All will be for naught. It's your plums they are after.

"Do you run your own business?" I tried hard to extract additional information from the guy.

"No," he said.

"Do you have money?" I said, digging deeper into the matter.

"No. You took everything I had."

"Do you have a house?"

"No," he said.

"Do you have anything at all?"

He spoke up, choking on his own tongue. "I look at you and I need no money, no house, no plums, no business. Nothing."

"You are crazy," I said.

"Yes, I am," he said.

"You are not worth a dime," I accused him.

"I'm not," he agreed.

"What will I do with you?" I wondered.

"Drink two glasses with me," he suggested.

Was it his tears or his daft answers that made his eyes shine like the sun and the moon?

"You are very pretty," he said.

We drank brandy, a glass, then a second one, and from then on, my dear girl, I know for sure: all men are stones. It's you who decides if you'll lug your man tied to your neck all your life or throw him in the mud and step on his head to keep your evening shoes clean.

There is yet another option: you'll drink two glasses of brandy with the guy, and like I did, you'll give birth to his children, all three of them pre-e-e-tty like the sun. And there's something else. Every time I look at the mirror, I say to myself, *He's judged correctly, yes, I'm pretty.*

Therefore, my dear, all men are stones, but only one among them is a precious stone. He is your man. The way he dresses makes you suspect he has bad taste in clothes. He is wild and, honestly, you don't think he has the skills to operate a business, but he is your gemstone. Take care of him.

Now, run to the nearest supermarket and buy a bottle of brandy. Two glasses are enough, not a drop more, not one!

I'm Cold

It was Thursday again and that meant at nine pm Becky Aneva's husband would visit her. He had emailed her, had called on her mobile, and had sent a fax message warning her to be in her bedroom exactly at that hour. Becky hoped that at least today she would break the established routine. Theo had some important, official meeting in Bonn and odds were that she would be in luck. He was already ten minutes late. She dreamt of going to Bonn herself. She loved the cold, humid air, the intimate fog hovering above squares and statues, the sluggish dark river, but above all, she enjoyed the closed faces of people. Their cool, unobtrusive presence put her at her ease. She was wind or dust on the sidewalk, and the feeling of solitude was sweet. She adored the loneliness of the houses. They were arranged in strict straight lines, each one had an ancient facade and a little fountain which spoke of the owner's frivolity. The marble arches cast their quaint shadows on the squares full of legends and history. She felt the stares of men on her skin; their parasite eyes delved deep into her flesh and sucked delicious juice from it.

Her husband's business partners were civilized enough, but Becky Aneva guessed that at the end of the day they had one of the expensive girls in their hotels. She imagined the services the men wanted and felt appalled. Thinking about men was an appalling occupation, for it made her remember Theo, her husband, and the Thursday nights he spent with her.

Becky hated Thursdays.

Bakalov, one of the business partners of Becky's husband, had so far behaved in a very friendly manner. He sent her discreet flower gift baskets on the mornings after each official dinner. At the last working lunch, the seventeenth in a long, tedious series, Becky mentioned something about the film *Titanic* just for the sake of participating in the conversation. Theo had warned her not to be silent like a statue even though she looked as beautiful as one. Out of pure politeness, Becky took part in the discussions. She dropped a question in the sphere of culture she had prepared beforehand — finance and politics were a perilous zone and Theo had cautioned her not to poke her nose in it, pointing out how narrow-minded her way of looking at things was. In general, he did his best to stress her overall inability to cope with anything outside cosmetics. Because of that, Becky asked Bakalov her well-prepared question, "Have you seen the film *Titanic*?" Perhaps the question was downright stupid but pronounced by her beautiful lips it acquired weight, and the businessmen, feeling the ennobling female presence, commented. Unlike all the rest of them who kissed her hand and bowed silently, the bolder ones discreetly directing their eyes down the neckline of her dress, Bakalov sent Becky a disc with the film.

Then he sent her a novel by Barbara Slow, an author Becky abhorred, so she paid her son's nurse, a woman called Arma, to read the novel and provide her with a two-page synopsis plus analysis of the basic story lines. Becky had made up her mind to indulge in a small adventure with Mr. Bakalov. She needed neither sex nor the sugary porridge of love. However, Bakalov attracted her with the fact that he had not lowered his eyes to the neckline of her dress, nor had he attempted to swim in the stream of the topic of how beautiful Becky was. He simply established a dear little tradition to send her modest bouquets of snowdrops on Mondays, Wednesdays, and Fridays. Becky appreciated them all the more because on these very days Di, the strange girl, came to her house and massaged her body with such intense concentration as if that was her favorite occupation in the world.

When Bakalov brought Becky to his villa in the country she saw him naked. The iceberg of repugnance hit her throat. Becky did not want Bakalov. She imagined his hands, scraggly, overgrown with transparent hairs, touching her. Then she saw his thin colorless lips closing on her mouth, and she thought she would throw up. Bakalov caressed her and Becky was scared by his dry palms moving rapidly all over her, his unnaturally quick fingers planting warts in her skin as they touched her. The experience was more unpleasant because of the question that Bakalov constantly kept asking her, "Does it feel good?"

Finally, Becky answered that it felt good, hoping that he would calm down, but he sank into her more intensively leaving dry pain in his wake. There were thin grooves of saliva running from the corners of his mouth on which Becky concentrated. Yet, she could gain considerable advantage from this situation. Bakalov's blue, almost transparent eyes swam in fog, his eyelids slid downwards, his mouth kissed her persistently as his body swayed on her like a buoy tied at the bottom of the sea. She could examine him closely and had the chance to experiment with him. She scratched his back, ready to avenge herself on his body for the humiliation and the splitting ache he gave her. Then she hit him.

Last Thursday night, while her husband Theo was making love to her, she scratched him as well. He hit her. That was the only time he had ever done that to Becky and after, when he had gone, the money left on the bed for the week was three times more than usual. From that time on, Becky suspected he nurtured a vein of sneering and sadistic malice. He tried to humiliate her in public and since she was not a woman given to procrastination and suspicions, she told him plainly, "Next time you hit me you're asking me for a divorce."

"You won't divorce me," Theo answered, his gray eyes hungry for her. "You need my money."

Becky didn't object and did not explain anything.

"Try me," she said.

***

Becky scratched Bakalov's back again, but instead of leaving her alone he blurted out, "You are great, you are great." He sounded credible as if he really believed what he said. His saliva dripped on her breasts and she hated that, but the exhilarating feeling that she was a researcher experimenting with a species unknown to science never left her. She could push and scratch and beat and bite him. She could do anything to him and for a moment, Becky was sorry her imagination was so poor she could not invent anything twisted and deviant.

"Stop," Becky ordered him. He ceased moving and sat up, whitish and undulating in his glass jar of acid where the tapeworms were preserved in her biology lab at school.

"I love you," Bakalov said, but Becky saw his shiny saliva and the whitish hairs piercing his colorless skin. "I love you. Marry me. Abandon your husband!"

She hit him once again, this time on the mouth, and instead of yelling, he tried to kiss her. Becky imagined the dark hands of the girl who massaged her and was unable to catch her breath.

Becky drove on the way back home and Bakalov slept, the streams of his saliva dripping onto the seat of his expensive car. She suddenly wanted to make him feel pain. Her desire was so irresistible that she drove her fingernails deep into his wrist. Bakalov woke up and looked around expecting that somebody wanted to break his neck. Becky stopped the car. It was so cold and wet that for a moment she wanted to throw Bakalov out in the street and go on without him. She kissed him instead and bit his lip, bit it savagely, feeling the taste of his blood in her mouth. He shouted with pain and as Becky let him go he whispered, "I love you."

Becky thought about the hands of the girl who massaged her and remembered that it was Thursday again. That meant that Theo would be home at nine p.m. His gray eyes—if the lewd gloss between his eyelids could be called eyes—would pick a spot on the floor, then he would order, "There!" Sometimes he didn't speak at all but it made no difference to Becky. She accepted his visits on Thursdays with the same reserve as her appointments with the dentist: the sooner they were over, the better. Theo didn't allow her to be a researcher intent on scratching, hitting and dissecting him closely. Very rarely, perhaps one Thursday a year, her husband would snort, "You are pretty, damn it."

"I'm cold," Bakalov muttered from the seat of his expensive car. "I am cold and I love you."

She had totally forgotten about him.

Pay Me

Theo watched the thin, long thread of a woman. The more he studied her face, the more he suspected she was not all there. The most amazing thing about her was her appetite. She constantly ate. They called her Maria. Damn it, such a beautiful name and such a big mouth, he thought. She worked part-time at the local library, washed staircases and mowed the lawns in front of the wealthy men's villas. He used an electric mower as loud as a gun. She cleaned the important ladies' houses and gave baths to the old women from the small town. Theo had heard rumors she was saving up to pay for her tuition at the local college.

She was different a fortnight ago. He caught glimpses of her a cup of coffee in hand, staring at a lanky, slovenly character. The man worked for Theo, repaired lathes and cutting machines, constantly complaining about too much dust, too hot, almost no money. Theo fired him.

Theo was intrigued by her; it was her big mouth that fascinated him. He was building a dyers' workshop in town, and he hired her to clean the place. It was hard to believe how rapidly her hands moved, her fingertips neon signs glimmering intoxicatingly before his eyes. He underpaid her and she didn't protest, didn't even bother to count the money. Her eyes on his face, she asked, "Can I pick the wild sorrels around the dyers' workshop?"

"Yes. You can," Theo said. "But you'll pay me five *leva* for my sorrels, as a matter of fact, ten *leva*."

She didn't respond to that, didn't invite him to go drown himself. She had turned around as if he was not there. Standing by a manure heap, Theo, the man who owned half the houses in town, all fertile fields, and had opened a dyers' workshop, stared at her, and she didn't care.

"Hey. Wait," Theo shouted. Her blouse intrigued him. He knew she'd bought it for fifty cents from his second-hand shop. The thing was too big for her, but her back looked very active in it, a snake twisting and turning within the confines of the huge hems. So far, no man or woman had dared to turn their back on Theo.

"Nobody has introduced you to me," her big mouth said. "I don't see any reason why you should call me 'Hey.' One should glance at a manure heap for fear that he might step in it. She trampled on his shadow and her back, already a grown-up snake, retreated into the fog.

He saw her floundering in those enormous dresses from his second-hand shop. At times, she rummaged inside her bag, her fingers surprisingly thin and nimble, extracting nettles or sorrels, dock leaves, and lettuces. She grazed on them. She stuffed sorrels in her mouth, munching, plucking another handful, then another.

Theo pursued a new hobby: he shadowed her. He watched her walking away from the library in a new one-*leva* dress from his second- to twenty-second hand shop, squatting by the stone wall, pulling and plucking nettles. She would push them into her green bag, then chew raw dark-green leaves. A week passed, the sorrels grew coarse and hard, and she plucked horseradish, then goose-foot. He saw her picking grasses, masticating, chewing the cud until the first strawberries were ripe. Then she didn't carry the green bag on her back; she clutched a crate with strawberries instead, gobbling fruit like thunder. His neighbors said she worked well, cleaned for many families, washed the sick, talked to old women from the village for hours on end, dug their gardens, weeded flowerbeds, and planted green beans or peppers. They gave her strawberries. She didn't want money. She looked around all the time as if she was searching for somebody.

Then the cherries were ripe.

That grumbling character she'd been staring at had vanished without a trace. Theo had a nagging doubt in the back of his mind: Maria started gorging on green leaves the day the shabby blighter beat it for some unknown place.

Theo owned the cherry orchard. He'd bought it dirt cheap, then he built huge walls that encircled the land and the trees. Nettles sprouted in the shadows which she, a stick in a bleached dress, picked and wolfed day and night.

"I want you to pick cherries," Theo said one day as Maria thrust a bunch of nettles into her green bag. "Twenty *leva* per day plus all fruit you can eat."

On the following day, she came in a T-shirt from his shop, shorts from his shop, her thin legs a pair of nails driven in her threadbare shoes which, he was sure, pinched her feet terribly. He hid behind the wall and watched. In the course of two hours, Maria had not stopped eating. Her lips turned bluish with cherry juice, and he was convinced she wouldn't do the job he'd hired her for. He was wrong. At a certain point, her fingers plunged into the foliage and her body stuck to the branches like resin. In the afternoon, Theo couldn't believe his eyes when he saw thirty crates of the cherries she'd picked.

"I'll pay you," he said.

She didn't look up.

"You said 'all the fruit you can eat.'" Her eyes were on her old shoes. "We agreed."

"We did," he said.

"I'll eat now," she said.

Theo sat in the shadow as she squatted on her heels, grabbed at a crate of cherries and ate, ate, ate as if she were a plant louse, a silkworm, her endless throat about to guzzle the whole orchard, the tree roots, the stones, the leaves, and the clouds above them. She chewed for an hour, then chewed more. Her mouth was black with the cherries, and her hands and elbows were crimson. Without warning, she jumped to her feet, vigorous, strong, as if she had just caught a glimpse of the orchard. She was a tapeworm that had pumped a ton of fruit into her flat belly. Theo thought, *now I know*. When the lanky character, dark like dried mud, hung around town, Maria didn't rummage for food. A cup of coffee was about all she'd had for breakfast.

"Pay me," she said.

He gave her fifteen *leva*.

"Give me five *leva* more," she said.

"You gobbled a load of my fruit."

"We cut a deal. Twenty *leva* per day and all I can eat."

"You ate too much," he said. "Come again tomorrow."

When Theo checked the orchard on the following day, he found her in another cherry tree, her mouth already black, her hands, forearms, and elbows red. He could see no cherries in the trees she had climbed yesterday. No crates full of cherries in sight.

"How much have you munched so far?" he asked.

Maria didn't say anything. In the evening, the same thing happened all over again. The cherry tree picked full and clean, the crates neatly arranged by the trunk, and she, glued like a caterpillar to the leaves of another tree, was eating slowly, quietly, obstinately, lost in thought as if solving an equation in nuclear physics.

He paid her ten *leva*.

On the following day, he found Maria in the largest tree. The sun had just regained its power in the sky, a dash of rays followed by the stupendous full stop of the summer day. When did she clamber up that tree? he wondered. Had she used a torch to illuminate the cherries, or had she slept up on a big branch?

Her mouth was purple, her forearms glowered, blue up to the elbows, and the cherry stones she had spat on the ground glittered like pearls. She was scrawny, a knife stuck in the bough. In the evening, the full crates waited for him, neatly arranged in two parallel rows. Again, she ignored Theo as he stood under the tree inspecting her work. Without warning, her shabby dress slipped down from the branch, crept to the crates and the thing started all over again. She ate, ate, ate as if she was about to devour the night and the dark road, the potholes on it, the old rusty boneshakers, the gray houses in the village, the donkeys tied with chains to metal stakes. He gave her five *leva*. Maria didn't say anything as she turned the snake of her back on him and went away, a firefly in the muggy air, a shaving razor that had learned to walk. She had cut him, and he didn't know where the wound was. He remembered that a month, maybe two months ago, her eyes carved the street, pushed him and hurried, then gave in, meek and tractable, swimming to that repulsive character's face.

"I ask you to dinner," Theo told her. He hadn't intended to ask her anything.

"Tomorrow," she said.

Her voice, full of stones, hit him in the face.

All the cherries were already ripe. He paid the women from the nearby villages since they had worked hard, and there was nothing to pick anymore. He fired a worker if she'd snapped a branch, so the orchard was stronger and more beautiful than ever. All clouds and blackbirds flew somewhere else.

In the evening, after the windows of the library darkened, Maria showed up at his door in the endless dress from his shop, in the same dusty dented shoes that pinched her. Theo had the feeling his stinking warehouse, with the sacks of threadbare clothes, was advancing on him. She had not bothered to put on makeup, no nail polish. His presence failed to impress her—Theo wasn't even a manure heap. He was nothing.

"Will you pay for the dinner?" Maria asked.

"Yes."

"No matter how much I eat?"

"That's correct."

The waitress came, a pretty girl Theo had spent a couple of unimpressive nights with.

"Trout with walnuts," ordered the shaving razor with a big mouth. "Turkey chops with honey, tomato salad, baked peppers, grilled chicken, fish, rye bread, wheat bread, cream salad, ice cream, apple pie, yogurt with almonds and honey for dessert, and some chocolates."

Theo listened to her, staring, rubbing his ears. They itched.

Then, she very slowly started to eat: the tomato salad, the turkey chop, the rye bread, fish and almonds, yogurt, the grilled chicken, the ice cream. She didn't look at him, not once, didn't glance at the waitress, the couple of unimpressive nights, who was gaping at her awe-struck, terrified. Maria ate on, sipping at the yogurt with honey, then bit into the turkey chop, and the moment the plate in front of her was empty, she pushed it away. She didn't talk to Theo, she ignored him. He was a bone of the trout she had just spat out. She ate beautifully, her hands flashing, a needle embroidering flowers on a baby's scarf in the dusk. The air turned into a tapestry of flames in the wake of her fingers.

After the last plate in front of her was empty, she carefully rubbed her fingers with the napkin and asked, "What do you want from me now?"

"You know what."

She stood up. He had no idea what she was going to do, turn the snake in her back and the endless dress on him or … he could not imagine what waited behind her. He didn't need to know. She started for his house. Young and old gasped for air, praising Theo's castle, the exquisite white bird, perched on the hill, surrounded by vineyards, grapes and wild foliage, a magnificent alley and marble benches in the shadows. She walked by his side, paying no attention to him, and that was odd. Theo had spent uninspiring nights with girls from the town, girls whose nationality he didn't bother to establish. None of them had kept mum like this one. He had fired the dark grumbling blighter. The man disappeared, had dried up like a muddy puddle that time erased from the sidewalk. It was on the day he was gone when Maria bought her green bag for twenty-five cents from Theo's notorious shop.

She took off her twentieth-hand enormous dress, oblivious to everything around her as if she was in her cluttered room or was about to dive into a muddy pool in the river.

The second they finished, she got off the bed, made no fuss, did not dillydally or smoke. She slipped on the huge sleeves, like a noose on her arms, and left. The night was memorable. Indeed, it was; the darkness a memory of the shaving razor that had cut him into two halves, her thin hands stitching together a Theo he didn't know. The warm midnight and her enormous dress made his head spin. On the following day, he went to the library. Maria sat at a battered desk, the green bag full of sorrels and a crate with raspberries like a sentinel at her feet, her nose buried in a book. She looked up and said, "What can I do for you?"

The nightfall in her eyes said she had never met him, and she didn't have an enormous dress that had flowed with her strawberry skin into a little pool at his feet. The indifferent corners of her mouth had forgotten that her hands had sewn something with invisible stitches under his skin and Theo couldn't extricate himself from it.

"I ask you to dinner tonight."

This time she ordered mackerel with walnuts, veal stew, cream salad, potato salad, nettle soup, chicken soup, baked peppers, ice cream, chocolates, a pork chop, and an apple pie. The dinner was over and she didn't wait for him to lead the way to his room. Her dress was of a different color, dusty brown, enormous, hanging like a bleached tatter on the thin rope of her body. His second-hand shop offered the same garments in several shades of brown. The thing slid from her shoulders and parachuted into his territory, landing on the floor. She bent down, touched the shabby fabric and carefully folded it. She hadn't put on knickers, he saw. Maria stood in front of him, her glowing fish-skin a glowworm in the dusk. The night was so memorable he couldn't make out if it was a night or a day, a Sunday or a Tuesday, January or July. He went to sleep, and she stood up, dragged on her gown and left, not bothering to look back.

He couldn't drink his coffee in the morning and didn't eat his breakfast. He ran to the library, but it was still closed. He hurried to the small house where he'd been told Maria lived. She wasn't there. He saw her in the street, the green bag slung over her shoulder, the gigantic dress spilling out a mudslide at her toes.

"I ask you to dinner," he said.

As usual, she said nothing.

Theo stared at her scraggy neck. Her hands turned the air into sewing cotton and needles. Her feet burned the steps he hoped her worn-out shoes would make towards him. She had picked blueberries somewhere and her mouth was purple, her hands glowed red. Was it strawberries she'd eaten? he asked himself.

Theo sat at a small table in the restaurant and the girl with the two unimpressive nights made efforts to talk to him. He consulted his watch, the evening slowly thickened into complete darkness, slow heat for hopeless old men, hot hours. He got up and the girl with her two insignificant nights asked him where he was going. Did he want her to accompany him? Theo didn't answer.

Maria didn't show up.

In the morning, she was not in the library. He didn't find her in the small house where she lived. Her green bag, full of sorrels and nettles a week ago, lay on the threshold, folded neatly, empty.

Theo felt hungry. His stomach twitched inside him. He ate two smoked veal sandwiches and drank two cartons of milk. His hunger grew. His appetite hit him, he wanted to eat, to devour, to absorb food quickly in large amounts. Maria had gone. Maria's eyes had run dry. His bones ached from hunger. He ran to the warehouse. The crates were stored there. He bent down, stuffed strawberries into his mouth, gulped them down. He ate. He swallowed fruit, stems, and leaves. They had no taste. Maria. After an hour or perhaps two, he accidentally looked up at the small stained mirror nailed to the wall.

His hands and forearms were purplish-red, soiled with strawberry pips. A scarlet-brown crust of dried strawberry juice had plastered his nose, lips, and chin.

Maria.

Good Figure, Beautiful Voice

Hell found me!

Most of the time, I felt peaceful. I rarely talked to anybody. I had always lived in unstable silence, winters hurling snow and rain at my windows, passing unnoticed and unnecessary. My next-door neighbor thought I was a queer fish. I could tell that by the way she stared at me when she met me at the grocery store. I'd been living in the neighborhood for five months. I chose a room with a window to the north, tucked away down a narrow street. All the houses were small and you could scarcely see them in the fog. There was fog everywhere: on the roofs, in the trees, in my hair, and on my coat. The sun gave birth to fog instead of mornings.

I thought I was bad company so I kept myself to myself, going for interminable strolls in the wasteland surrounding the only bridge in town. I tried to remember the outlines of the low squat buildings as they slowly dissolved into the afternoons like memories of a snowstorm. Sometimes guys whistled at me. The town was not big. People knew each other but I was a stranger, a new poster advertising for a concert on the main street.

I guessed the townsfolk unanimously mistrusted me when they learned what I did for a living. Even before the end of the first month living on the narrow street, I gained a steady notoriety as an unbearable teacher of mathematics. I wanted the students to prove theorems and solve problems. I didn't speak much to them. Even on the first day of school, I caught two guys cribbing from finely folded sheets of paper they had tucked up their sleeves. The bad thing about me was that I saw and heard most of what happened in the classroom. I could almost always tell when a guy was trying to cheat. When I was a little girl, even Grandma could not trick me into believing that Dad had gone on a long business trip to Greece to make money for us. I knew he had divorced my mother. A year after that, I knew my mother would not come back home to see me as she had promised after uncle Ivan took her to the hospital for some blood tests. I tried to keep a stiff upper lip, but all I managed was to bite my lower one, which had long ago become very thin and colorless.

I only talked in the classroom. I hated to see guys copying from their neighbors. I took the neatly folded sheets of paper with the formulae from their fists and kept them on my desk. My classes hated me. I saw it in their eyes and everything I said seemed short, stiff and formal. Outside of class, I felt awkward every time I met a student sauntering by, the fog freezing me in front of the bridge near the wilderness.

One Wednesday, I asked one of the students to prove the theorem about raising the diagonals of a rhombus to the second power. I watched him closely as he tore the sheet from his textbook and started walking to the blackboard. He began to copy the theorem from the sheet, not even trying to conceal what he was doing. He printed the words slowly, unfalteringly, taking peeks at me behind his shoulder. I gave him a poor mark.

"Sit down," I said.

He remained in front of the blackboard, calm, tall, writing the formulae, his fingers sifting out the chalk powder. He copied the theorem to the end and bowed to the class. The students applauded vigorously, some laughing, others smirking. I didn't know what to do with my eyes and my hands. I panicked. I had dropped a piece of chalk some time ago and I saw it at my feet on the floor. It was very hot in the room. Words failed me, I stood there, egg on my face. I was scared my voice would sound gravelly and they all would dissolve into laughter. They watched on, perfectly silent. I staggered to the blackboard and gripped another piece of chalk, then started dictating slowly, the words dead on my lips, "The diagonals of a rhombus ..."

The students listened. I hoped they had not noticed how dry my voice was or perhaps they were accustomed to it that way. Suddenly, the boy I had given a poor mark jumped from his desk and sent his bag crashing to the floor.

"Excuse me," he said, strutted to my desk, took my piece of chalk, and left without closing the door.

All the rest were silent, watching me. I checked the boy's name in the register. Mikhail.

I had four more lessons that weighed a ton each. I felt squashed. In fact, every day I left school as exhausted as if I had dragged crags and stones from the slate-quarry in the hill to my living room. I had a headache. The schoolyard, shops, and birches were brown silhouettes, and the town was whispers and whirring of motors through which my headache and I walked. I reached my narrow street where the houses were neat and immobile mussel shells.

The small square in front of the cottage where I lived was my medicine. It ended abruptly at the foot of a hill overgrown with shrubs and thorns that mixed with the autumn and its starless sky. I wanted a cup of tea. I wanted my warm room where I could forget the classroom, the town, and the theorems. Every evening I lit all the lamps and celebrated the absence of fog and blackboards around me. I had counted the steps that separated my room from the schoolyard. It was fun counting the yards that I had to walk before my cup of strong tea.

Somebody whistled at me. I jumped. I rarely met people in my narrow street, silence there felt like the ocean floor. The face, which popped up in the mist before me, gave me the creeps. It was the student I had given a poor mark.

I walked slowly on, aware of strange noises. I soon realized there were two more guys I didn't know with Mikhail. I crept on, forbidding myself to turn back, feeling their words and breaths on my neck. I wasn't scared, not in the least. I could hear their light footfalls behind my back. When I was a little girl, my grandmother used to leave me at home by myself when she gave lessons in math to students at their homes. I was accustomed to silence and I knew it was my friend. The three guys stalked me, silent like the brown clouds. I had lived alone and I was not afraid of footsteps in the dark. I reached the front door of the house where I lived, turned around, and looked at them. They stared back. I entered the house and closed the door. Inside was quiet and warm.

On the following day, Mikhail walked out of the classroom in the middle of my lesson. He had been humming a familiar tune for quite a time. When I asked him to stop, he winked at the class, then left.

In the afternoon, Mikhail and the other two guys trailed after me while I walked along the street paved with gray clouds. I wished I could dash off, yet I wasn't scared. It was dark and I could hear their shoes hit the pavement. One of the three guys, the tallest among them with a swarthy face, caught up with me, halted, and looked me in the eyes.

"I'd like to tell you something," he said. "My name is Len." His face, long and thin, almost touched mine. He cleared his throat. "I have never met a girl like you. You have a good figure." His dark eyes measured me slowly. "You have a beautiful voice. Your eyes are beautiful."

A thick stream of derision oozed from his words. Mikhail and the other guy were only a step away from us, watching me, snickering. Len, the tallest one, snickered too. Then he let out a loud guffaw. I looked at him and then turned and continued down the street. The houses waddled in the dusk making it jagged and menacing. I reached the small square, the shrubs, and wilderness. This time my well-lit room and my cup of strong tea were no good.

In the morning, I had a headache that became excruciating during the five lessons with my classes. I dictated the problems and repeated the theorems, trying to ignore the waves of uneasiness as best as I could. Finally, the lessons were over and I walked slowly out of the school yard.

The three guys were waiting for me at the beginning of my narrow street. They roared with laughter the minute they saw me. I hurried past them, trying to remain composed.

"I'd like to tell you something," one of the guys shouted. I didn't stop. I noticed his eyes were the color of the fog—watery, cold. "I have never met a girl like you before. You have a good figure. You have a beautiful voice …" He was short of breath and looked at Mikhail and Len for support. I didn't wait for the remaining part of the explanation.

"Will Mikhail be the next one?" I asked.

My question was greeted with jeers. I ignored them. My eyes were beautiful, I knew that. I left the guys where they were, feeling their eyes watching my back as I walked down the narrow street. I went home and tried to sleep. The town was blue behind the windowpanes.

In the morning before I went to work, I found the three guys in the square with the bridge. Mikhail and Len came striding along to meet me.

"I'd like to tell you something," Mikhail said. Then he blushed and looked away.

"I won't listen to you," I told him.

"I have never met a girl like you," he said. "You have a good figure. Your voice is beautiful. And your eyes ..." He looked at the bridge for help, hoping I'd go away. I waited.

"Her hair is beautiful, too," Len whispered in Mikhail's ear. Len' words were sharp, cutting his face into two halves.

"Tomorrow I'll wait for you at 7:00 p.m. in front of my house," I said.

"She's up to something," Len muttered.

Perhaps my neighbor had seen me and was wondering what I was discussing with these young men. I took a step forward. I had to go to work.

"What did you say?" Mikhail asked.

I didn't answer.

"Hey, what did you say?" Len cried out, his voice indignant. "You'll wait for me, is that it?"

I didn't answer him. I had one thousand more steps before I reached the classroom.

"What did you say?" Len caught up with me.

"Tomorrow at 7:00 p.m.," I said, so quietly he had to bend to hear my words.

That day I examined many students. I spoke slowly, avoiding their eyes. I didn't look at Mikhail.

At 7:00 sharp I was in front of my house. Len had already arrived. The other two boys were a couple of yards away from him, hiding behind a clump of pine trees. This time they weren't laughing. They watched me. I watched them, too. I wasn't scared.

Len waited, his hands thrust into his pockets. I came up to him, nodded, studying his face. It was very smooth and dark. He kept silent as I watched him run his fingers through his hair. It was black and thick.

"Hi," he said at last.

The other two guys had pushed aside the branches of the pine trees. They waited, ready to start sniggering. Suddenly I hated them.

"Stop fidgeting," I told Len.

He stared, confused. I caught him by the shoulders, stood on tiptoes and kissed him.

I hated Mikhail and the other guy. I hated the man I had just kissed, and I couldn't stand the fog. I had already taken my revenge. No sound of steps chased me, no one guffawed. The fog and the pavement were peaceful. The houses smiled.

The next morning the classroom was quite peaceful. The students looked at me peculiarly, their eyes quiet like my evening cup of tea. As always, I started the lesson with a new theorem leaving a storm of chalk dust in my wake. Mikhail smiled. I stopped turning back to look at them.

When the lessons were over, Len waited for me near the bridge. His two friends were not with him.

The Clarinet

"Don't take my clarinet, Metto, please," Ivan said. "Do you remember when I played on it for your father? The old man's heart wasn't good, and his nerves were even worse. The nights gave him a nasty pain in the ribs. But I played him a song and he, well, you know what happened. He stretched himself out and limbered up. Look how battered the thing looks, Metto." Ivan wore a frazzled quilted coat and clutched an old clarinet in his hand. It was evident the musical instrument had been through a lot of trouble—there were scratches and cuts all over its faded surface.

"You've been buying on tick for months now, Ivan," the man behind the counter said. "You haven't paid me back a single dime."

The men were in a poky room, a café, a pub and a convenience store all rolled into one. Metto, its owner, sold the villagers rice, sugar and bread, which he drove from the town of Pernik in his pickup truck.

"I can't give your wife things on credit anymore. When I see her coming, I lie to her that it's time to close the shop."

"Listen, I'll play free of charge at your son's wedding," the man in the quilted coat said, fingering the lusterless keys of the clarinet. "I'll play for free at the weddings of all your cousins, and I'll play for free at the funerals of all the old men in your clan. If you open a new shop or a new pub, I'll play for nothing, gratis. You'll see. Send for me in the dead of night and I'll waste no time. I'll run over to your place like a rocket and I'll start performing. I can play at a wedding and I can play at a funeral. I can play for your new pub and for your old pub. Don't take my clarinet away. My son's learning to play now. The boy's got a sharp ear and strong lungs. He catches sounds from the streets and puts them in the instrument."

"You shouldn't drink so much, man. Why didn't you find a job in Italy? You should've made money instead of blabbering on about your kid," the tavern keeper said reaching towards the clarinet. "My son's young. He won't get married soon, and if my father dies, a dozen of bad eggs like you will turn up to play at his funeral just for the free beer, you know."

"Nobody can play like me, Metto," the clarinetist said. "You know that."

It was cold in the room and the tile stove smoked. The smell of burnt logs mingled with the vapors of smoldering plastic bottles. Metto wasn't a wastrel. He'd burn anything that he could burn to keep his shop warm. Rumors had it that he bought dead men's clothes and put them in the stove to save firewood in winter.

"When you threw a birthday party for your son, I played for him, free of charge and your wife cried," Ivan, the clarinetist, said. "And your father recovered after I played for him, although the doctor said the old man was just about to meet his maker. When the dentist pulled out your bad tooth, didn't you ask me to come and play for you? You were swollen like a bagpipe, but I played for you, and I killed the pain."

"You killed the pain because we got drunk together." Metto cut him short. "And before you were done, you had sucked a bottle of my best brandy dry. Did you pay for it? No, you didn't give me a penny to bless myself with," the pub keeper muttered and reached out to collect the clarinet. "Look at it. It's fit for the junk-heap. Did you use that clarinet to dig in your garden with or what?" The pub keeper shook his head in disgust. "I wonder who I can sell it to. What else can I take from you, Ivan? Your TV rattles as if all its screws are loose. You can't even make out what you are seeing — a cow or a submarine."

"You can take ... do you want me to give you my fridge?"

"That used to be my fridge, man. I threw it out and you went and collected it. I don't want the damn fridge."

"Then take the table from our kitchen. It's almost new. What do you say to that?" Ivan asked his voice strong with a new hope. "I'll put boards in the kitchen. The missus and I will make do with the boards. The kid's learning to play the clarinet now. He can play at weddings and he can play in your new pub. It would be a pity to take the thing away from him. He might become a big musician. He might play at the funerals of the big shots. His mother will cry her eyes blind if she sees that he has nothing to play on."

"I wouldn't drink like an eel if I was that interested in my son's dabbling with music. If I wanted my son to play at the funerals of the big shots, I wouldn't be bone idle like you, man. In the morning, your wife came to buy milk on tick. She already owes three months' salary to pay off her debts. What if her boss fired her? What if the dressmaking shop she works for went bust?"

"You can't sell my clarinet to anybody, Metto. It's ancient. It belonged to my grandfather, you know. He played on it in Bucharest, Romania, and in Athens, Greece. Then my father played on it in Sofia for the miners and in Pernik, at Easter. I ... I've played on it only here, in our village. Man, I tell you, who heard my tunes he forgot he was sick. Your own father—"

"No way. It's no use talking. What else can I take from you?" the café owner grumbled. "You are a loafer and a shirker. I'll nail that clarinet to the wall. Your grandfather and your father played on it. You drank it away. You know why some guys don't know chalk from cheese. It's because they drink. Their wives buy everything on credit, and before they are done they have spent three months of their pay!"

"Can I come here in the evenings"' Ivan asked, unbuttoning his quilted coat. "I'll take the clarinet down, and I'll play for a couple of minutes, no more."

"Do I look crazy to you? You'll scare away my clientele."

At that point, the door of the pub opened and a boy, scrawny and weak, shorter than the counter in the pub, entered and joined the men.

"Like father like son," the pub keeper muttered. "Manno, go tell your mother I can't sell her sugar on tick anymore. Your father will leave the clarinet here and I'll give you bread for five more days. That's all."

The boy was silent. His eyes sank into the floor and remained there. Then he fumbled in his pockets, produced some small change, four cracked glass balls, a sling, and a clean handkerchief.

"Uncle Metto," the boy began. "Take all these. Are they enough to buy Dad's clarinet back? This is the best sling in the village. And those are the hardest glass balls in the neighborhood. You can buy a bar of *Milka* chocolate on those nickels here. You only have to add forty-two cents and the bar of *Milka* will be yours."

"No way, Manno. Go home," the pub keeper said, scratching his head. Then he gave the boy a chocolate. "Take this, lad, and go home to your mother. There's a nip in the air. Run or you'll catch a very bad cold."

The boy fingered the chocolate, added it to the cracked glass balls, the sling, and the coins. He then took off his hat, hand-knitted with thick home-spun wool, added it to the rest of his possessions, and said, "Will you give me the clarinet now? Those things should be enough. And I'll come to sweep your pub first thing in the morning. Dad can play at your son's wedding free of charge. I mean when your son Dancho grows up. Dad can play at your father's funeral for free. I don't want Grandpa Boris to die, you know ... I mean ... I quite like him."

"Go home, Manno," the pub keeper said mildly.

"Let me play the clarinet for a couple of minutes," the boy said. "Let me play then I'll bring our dog Rexi. I'll give him to you and you'll give me Dad's clarinet."

The pub keeper gave the boy the battered instrument which had played in Bucharest, Romania, and in Athens, Greece. It had played at all weddings and funerals in the village as well. The boy took it.

"Uncle Metto," he said. "If your heart hurts, have no fear. It'll stop hurting after you hear me play. I promise."

It was cold in the pub. The freezing wind howled outside and the air in the room smelled of burned plastic, cigarette smoke, and smoldering beech firewood.

Quiet sounds trickled from the old clarinet, very soft ones, like the steps of a man who had recuperated from a long illness. Like the voice of a child who found a terrific penknife in the street. Like Athens, Greece, where the sun always shone, and like Bucharest, Romania, where it was winter now, but it was good all the same because in the houses the stoves burned and there was enough firewood; like sugar in your tea, like bean soup when you are hungry like a wolf. Like your mother's three salaries that she had not earned yet; like the two terrific glass balls and the best sling in the village. Like the wedding of Uncle Metto's son who'd grow up after twelve years. Like wedding guests who drank a glass or two and were ready to dance till their heels burned. The lad's clarinet wouldn't stop until the oldest grandpa jumped and danced with the young girls.

Finally, the boy stopped playing and the old clarinet once again looked battered and bruised. It seemed it had never seen Athens and Bucharest. It looked as though the hands of Ivan's father had never touched it, nor had the hands of Ivan who, to be honest, drank like a fish. Now the clarinet knew only about Ivan's debts.

The pub-keeper was not looking at the bottles on the counter. He didn't see the packets of sugar, and the big sacks of beans and rice. He didn't notice the stove in which the empty plastic bottles burned.

"Boy," the pub keeper said, "take your clarinet and run back home. Tell your mother I'll bring you bread for one week. It will be on me. It's my treat. You play really great, boy!"

His Cold Skin and the Snakes

I felt good in the room that faced the wall of the old house decorated with sculptures of snakes and half-naked men. When my translation didn't go well I stared at their taut muscles. Yet, I was quite happy when Stavro visited my office. He was a queer fish; he maintained that the gloom inside him blended well with the dusk in the room. He said he was not afraid of death in my office. In the shadows of the men on the opposite wall he felt he was a man himself. He admitted he feared his mother, who wholeheartedly disapproved of me. He feared loneliness and headaches. He hinted he was afraid even of me, but he locked the door and kissed my lips.

In the evenings when we sat together in front of the low-spirited television, he said he could love me only in the office, before these men and snakes. It was dark when I translated short stories, the characters in them gliding over chutes of twilight around dictionaries that knew everything in the world worth knowing. While I translated, Stavro sat by my side, watching, my scarf wrapped around his neck. At times, he grabbed my hand. We didn't make love, but he locked the door all the same. We held hands, his fingers cold like the blue wind, his eyes lonelier than the empty tramways. Often, he let me go and wrote rhymes, black poems on scraps of paper which he thrust into my pockets, into my stockings, into the only vase I had. He put his best poems on my heart to make me feel them the way they deserved. I seldom read them. They were heaps of words, no commas, no paragraphs, verbs, interspersed with capital letters, which didn't make clear if Stavro loved me or he had a stomach ache because of his fear of death. He left his poems in my shoes, glued them onto the walls and dedicated them to the part of my body he loved best. I said that made me hate poetry.

He stuck his ear to my heart and listened, his cold skin and the snakes entering my bones. He and the corners in my office despised the characters in the short stories I translated. He thought I loved them more than him.

Stavro's mother said her son was going mad in that office which she had found for me. When I worked outside Sofia, Stavro waited for me in the cafe opposite and took me to dinner at his parents' place. His mother, the famous psychiatrist, sat at the far end of the table, away from his father, a famous psychiatrist, too. He chose one of the corners to which light had almost no access at all. Stavro had told me his father slept in a separate room, the one with heavy velvet curtains hanging on either side of the huge window I admired so much. Dr. Yaneva, the mother, switched on a powerful lamp to illuminate her splendid hair. She often gave me brochures on various pomades, moisturizers and hair softeners, which I translated into Bulgarian for her.

Stavro told me once he detested female hair and asked me to cut mine as short as possible. His parents had provided me with an apartment above their own, and Stavro complained that he could feel the light of his mother's hair pierce our floor and creep onto the carpet. Like his father, he obstinately had his hair cut every ten days and shaved meticulously, his beard wicked and vindictive because of his desire to totally erase it. He had chosen thick, purple brocade curtains for his windows. Occasionally, he woke me in the dead of night when ghostly taxies whizzed along the streets, and said, "I love you." That meant he wanted me to go to my office to love me. There, the characters in the stories lay between the pages of my dictionaries like dry leaves in an herbarium. Sometimes we ran twice a night to my office, to the twilight and the half-naked men.

Our dinners were quiet, Stavro and his father withdrawn in the shadow of the curtains. I wondered how it was possible for them to find their mouths with the forks in that darkness. I preferred to remain flooded by the light of Dr. Yaneva's splendid hair, although she constantly interrogated me about the cheese and the kind of sex I liked, what my phobias were and what I thought of the Minister of National Health, a man I didn't know at all, a fact that bitterly disappointed her. Once, Dr. Yaneva and I went shopping together. After our first attempt at that, I came to hate all fashion centers. She was a Napoleon there and made a point of getting the highest compliments on everything she had, including the wart on her elbow, an item she desperately tried to eradicate. She had already spent a fortune on that. I told her how beautiful she was but that wasn't enough. I failed to convince her she was breathtaking and I developed a violent headache. I thought the woman's resentment against me stemmed from my inability to explain things to her. She inquired after my former boyfriends, emphasizing that they all posed a major threat to her son, whose heart I was bound to break. She asked me what I thought of her husband, of whom I thought nothing. Despite that, we had a cup of coffee. At a certain point, she sobbed and uttered a spiral of words that got wet and glistened like diamonds. She said she had come across a weird text amongst the medical papers of her husband's patients. In that text, her husband often mentioned my name. There were diagnoses of psychotic disorders as well, but the fact he had written *breasts* in Latin made her suspect that her husband sadly had fallen for an inappropriate person. She asked me not to come to dinner at their place anymore.

In the evening, Stavro's father came to my office and asked, staring at the curtains of purple brocade, if he could please wait for his son here while I translated a short story about two drunks who attempted to drown in the swimming pool of the woman they were both in love with. He said my office was a beautiful place, so quiet, and so dark. Then he sat on a stool and waited while the two drunks were out boozing, savoring the vintage, making no mention of the woman who had caught their fancy.

The psychiatrist sat on his stool covered with purple brocade, staring rigidly above my head. After half an hour of that, he rose, said, "See you later, Sonya." He left me like the characters in the short story who didn't get drowned because their wine was much better than that woman ... because they could live perfectly well without her.

Then Stavro came and said he wanted to kiss me, which he didn't do. Like his father, he sat on that stool and stared at the same spot, somewhere above my head. At a certain point, he produced a bottle and drank from it. I knew Stavro was no good at drinking. He coughed, then softly shed tears like the half-naked men, like the snakes that crept lovingly to me. I didn't ask what was wrong. He had cried like that once because he loved me. His love was stronger than him, he said, and he didn't know what to do with it. Tears turned his body into thin dusk, into a cloudy sky under my fingers.

"I'll move into your place if you want me to," Stavro said, his words staggering through half-dried tears. "I can't stand my parents."

He touched my hand, his fingers cold with the night behind the curtains. I love you, said the night in his fingers. I didn't know what I could give him when he added he was hungry.

He looked hesitantly at the hamburger bun which remained from my lunch, then asked me to hold the stale slice of bread.

"You'll always hold my food in your hands. When you touch it, it becomes delicious, delicious ... delicious!"

I touched an apple, an old croissant, and a chocolate. He ate them all, loved me more than the world again. There was no more food I could touch. He kissed me and said he wanted to sleep in the old easy-chair under the purple curtain. I should be around, breathing all the while, because if I went away his stomach hurt, just below his ribs, on the left-hand side.

That night I slept in the lumber room. There was the original bed in which Stavro's mother spent the night after she earned her Ph.D. When time came for me to go to the bed of his mother's Ph.D. thesis, he pressed himself, cold like the book about the two drunks, against my back.

I was hungry, so hungry I could eat the old stool, but I could not extricate myself from his embrace. He believed that without me he'd choke on the smell of his mother's Ph.D. thesis in the lumber room. At a certain point, he forced a bundle of banknotes into my hand. The money was his father's.

"Give that to Sonya," the doctor had said. "She's lost weight. She's become transparent like the glass cabinet with tranquilizers in my clinic. Tell her to buy better food."

I held the sausages I had brought in my hands and they, Stavro said, became rich in vitamins, half-naked men and snakes. Stavro's eyes were brocade curtains that turned their windows to me. He didn't want me to be those transparent tranquilizers in his father's clinic. He didn't want me to live for the sake of the weird characters in the shorts stories he hated.

The bottle of apricot brandy he had bought to keep us warm in the blizzards of January remained open by the stool, filling the darkness with gorgeous apricot trees, blossoms, and squirrels. If you killed a squirrel that ate your apricots, you were bound to be unlucky in your love; you wouldn't be able to conceive a child; men would stop thinking about women and would care only about men. But that happened only if you killed a squirrel that had eaten your apricots and had drunk from your apricot brandy.

I couldn't fall asleep. The smoldering fireplace of the night behind the dictionaries sparked alive with squirrels and apricot brandy. Stavro was gone and I pulled back all the curtains in the office, the blue ones in the lumber room, letting the clouds, the naked men and snakes watch me. I wouldn't have any windowpanes if I could, I even wouldn't have walls. I would sleep with January and the snakes.

Somebody entered my office.

Perhaps that was Stavro who felt despondent about the dazzling lamps along the boulevard, or perhaps the cars' headlights depressed him. They often did. He'd leave my place but the headlights would just be unbearable, so he'd ask me to walk him home. I was his protective curtain of purple brocade, he said.

"Sonya!" that was his father's voice, transparent like his glass cabinet, a quiet voice that predisposed his patients to calm down. I calmed down, too. "It hurts, Sonya," he said, pointing at a spot under his ribs. "I am hungry, but I am scared to eat."

I said nothing. I, too, would be scared to eat if that spot in my stomach under the ribs hurt me. He gave me a small loaf of white bread. That seemed strange. His wife bought only rye bread to keep the whole family slim.

"Please, hold the bread, Sonya."

I took the loaf which was as white as the moon and he watched me, or perhaps he watched the moon. At last, he bent and I could not imagine what he was about to do.

He started eating, chewing carefully, swallowing shreds of fine white bread, his eyes wide. It appeared his gaze propped up the roof of that old house.

He ate a long time, maybe an hour, until nothing was left. He didn't say anything. Suddenly, his lips brushed against my cheek, cold January lips, smelling of the moon. Then he was gone.

Before he closed the door, I caught a glimpse of a woman. Her hair shone in the light of the lamp. The woman sobbed softly, her tears as soft as breadcrumbs.

The Yellow Bag

I had been watching John for a month now. He was tall and scraggly, and his shirt was so old there was no color left in it. He spoke little and his eyes were dark and quiet. I didn't know why they frightened me. They were full of nights and cold winds, those eyes. He mowed the peasants' meadows and built their barns; he killed their pigs at Christmas and cleaned their backyards. He lived in a deserted cottage far from the other houses in a dell overgrown with nettles and elder trees. I thought his place looked beautiful when it rained, for when it rained John sang. I crept near the open window of his room and listened. In my mind, his voice was bigger than the night with the freezing wind and the black clouds in it. Other villagers, too, sneaked near his place. The harder it rained the bigger his voice was. There was a question I'd wanted to ask John. His cap was ancient, his trousers were soiled and frayed, and his shoes were torn but he always carried a yellow bag on his back. It was quite a big thing, and it was clean. A clean yellow bag, a torn shirt, old shoes and unshaven face: that was what John was. I was scared to ask him what he carried in his bag. When he sat down to eat his meager lunch, a chunk of cheese and bread, he carefully laid the yellow thing by his side eying it as he chewed.

I had asked most of my neighbors in the village about that bag. No one knew anything. My best friend Dina thought he carried brandy in it and she said I was crazy to like a man who most probably was not all there.

"I don't like him," I said. "I'm just curious."

The whole village knew what happened when I said I was just curious. The thing I was curious about vanished and no one found it again. I stole the thing. The cellar of my house was clean and well swept. I stored the swiped items elsewhere, in Dina's attic. Or I threw them in the shallow gorge where the river flowed as thin as a pencil.

"Don't," my best friend Dina said. "He might need it."

I was afraid of the dead moons in John's eyes and at the same time, I felt like having them all to myself.

"What's in your bag?" I asked one day.

It was the first time that I had spoken to him. He stopped and looked at me. His eyes were distant, lusterless. He wasn't listening to me.

"If you don't tell me what you carry in that bag, I steal it from you," I said.

He didn't say anything.

"I'll steal it from you and I'll burn it," I looked him straight in the eye and I was not sure he understood.

"I mean it," I whispered, wanting to hit him, and hit him hard.

"I carry my soul in the bag," he said. His voice was deep and rich, and it made me jump.

"What?"

"You heard me," he repeated.

"Oh, come off it," I almost shouted.

It was hot and I thought the blazing sun had made the man go crazy. "My soul's big. It's too narrow for it inside me," he said then he left me in the hot bristling afternoon and climbed the hill to his dilapidated cottage, to the nettles and elder trees I liked so much.

"What did he tell you?" My friend Dina asked itching to learn the secret and spread the word about it far and wide.

"You wouldn't like to know," I said.

She was silent for a while; she knew me well and she did everything I told her to do. That was the only reason I had not sent her packing. I hated nosy neighbors and I had a good way of getting rid of them. My relatives and friends that didn't mind their own business and poked their noses in mine lost something precious: a coat, a ring, or a watch they treasured. Everybody suspected me; no one had ever caught me red-handed. I got on with guys who obeyed what I told them to do. The ones who didn't lost items they held most dear and lost them for good. If a bloke felt like breaking with me he gave me all I wanted first. If he didn't, he lost all anyway. Often something unexpected occurred: a barn burning or the engine of a car dead. Other unpleasant things happened, too. That was all.

The day John came to mow Dina's meadow he carried his clean yellow bag on his back.

"Can I see what your soul looks like?" I asked.

I had long waited for him to mow Dina's meadow.

"No," he said.

Then he went his way staring straight ahead as if I was an old bench or a heap of dead leaves on the ground. I'll teach you to respect a thief, I thought. I'll show you.

In the afternoon, I sneaked to John's hut. I sat on the wooden bench and waited for him. I was surprised how neat the only room was. There was a bed, a table and a box which was not locked. Two more shirts, both frazzled and bleached was all there was in that box. I searched the place and I found nothing of interest. It felt as though no one lived in that clean empty place. There was no food, no drinking water. No underwear, no household items, no linen. Did John really live here? I asked myself.

He didn't seem to be surprised to see me sitting on his bench, in his room.

"I brought you some leek soup," I said.

He didn't even look at me.

"What's in your bag?" I grunted after he sat on the bed, distant and silent.

"You know what it is," he said. "I've told you it is too narrow for it inside me," he stared at me as if I had not already heard that lie.

"Let me see it."

"No way."

He ate the soup I'd brought.

"Thank you," he said. "Now go."

"I don't want to go."

But when he lay on the bed and yawned, I left the room. You don't know me, I'll show you, I thought. I peeped through the keyhole and saw him thrust the bag under his frayed shirt. Okay, I could wait long enough. When I looked through the dirty window he had drifted to sleep. Slowly and noiselessly, I opened the door. I had prudently taken grease to make the rusty hinges as silent as an empty purse. I tiptoed to his bed, reached out, extracted the clean yellow bag out of his shirt and slipped soundlessly to the door. He didn't budge. His breathing was even and deep. I'd expected he would snore, that thin tall man. The bag was as light as a box of matches. I pressed it close to my chest as I padded out of the room. Outside, the nettles and the leaves of the elder trees were all wet with the rain. The clouds in the sky moved slowly like camels of a lost caravan, and the old gossip, the wind, hissed to the trees. I didn't mind the cold.

Our village was a small one, a dozen of houses at the bottom of a shallow valley which to me looked like a cauldron surrounded by steep slopes and bald craggy peaks. At the bottom of the cauldron, our nameless river flowed, as thin as a pencil in summer and bigger than the sky in the autumn. I loved its nameless cutting water. Looking at it made me think of my childhood, the puny child I was: thin like a pencil, and as sharp and brittle. My mother said she'd go to buy me a doll but bought me nothing. As a matter of fact, she didn't come back home. I heard my cousins say she ran off with the guy who came to mow our meadow. That was what our village was: a place where men came to mow the meadows. Those men never went away alone. They took a woman from the village with them, and a child remained at the windowpane waiting for a pretty little doll. Then Dad said he'd buy me a dog, but I knew he wouldn't come back. I'd noticed he'd taken his heavy rucksack with him. Even my cousins didn't know whom he ran off with. Maybe he simply drank too much and that day the nameless river, as big as the mountain, had taken him. He had told me it was a shame to cry.

I couldn't open the yellow bag. Its strings were fastened too tightly. They couldn't scare me. I always carried a sharp knife on me.

I was a happy child. I built shallow pools in the river, and I told the fish fairy tales. I had no one else to tell them to. It was on the river bank that I had stolen a skirt for the first time. It had been so easy. I thought it was unfair my grandmother should punish me after she saw me with the big stolen skirt on. She should have said I was such a nimble-fingered girl. No one of the dozen women saw me pilfer the thing. Grandma forbade me to go to the pool for a month instead, and I learned my lesson. I had to burn the things I stole. What wonderful light the burning stolen trousers, bags and gloves gave.

The yellow bag had long straps I failed to untie. Well, my knife was as sharp as dog's fangs. I whetted its blade every week ever since Dad went out to buy me a puppy. That blade was the reason why the village respected me.

The yellow leather was thick and strong. I worked hard for an hour before I cut out a small hole in it. Then I peeked inside. The thing I saw looked like a sponge. It was so white I suddenly felt dizzy. I pushed my little finger through the narrow opening and pressed the sponge. Its surface was cold to the touch. It felt very smooth. Then I cut and pulled at the leather until the slit was big enough to insert my hand into the bag. Something had happened. The sponge was no longer there. The thing I touched was either a stone or a slab of ice. I looked inside; the stone was black. A minute before it had been dazzlingly bright.

I hit it with my fist.

A cry of pain flew from the run-down hut. I recognized John's voice.

I stood in my tracks. John's voice was so beautiful.

Then I remembered. When Grandma punished me, I went to the pool I'd built and I told it I hated her. That was not true. She gave me bread and she told me tales. She had taught me everything I knew.

"When you come to the river at night, you'll see," she said. "The pool mirrors the stars. They are all yours."

The starts in the pool were tiny like bread crumbs, and the moon was a silver quince. I drank the water from the pool and I drank the stars and the night in it. Maybe that was why I saw nights in John's eyes. I'd drunk so many cold moons I could recognize them when I saw them in someone's eyes.

I scratched the black stone in the bag with my nails.

One more cry of pain sank into the cold afternoon.

I seized the bag, ran back to John's hut and hurled the yellow thing inside. A dark heavy ball fell onto the floor, thudded and rolled under the table. I didn't know what happened after that. I ran and ran until I could no longer breathe.

In the evening, I cooked leek soup.

I missed my grandmother. I missed her so much. She was dead and the moons she had told me fairy tales about shone no more. I didn't cry. I thought of the water I had drunk hoping I wouldn't be so lonely after I had moons and stars in me. Dina was not my best friend. A friend didn't obey you, a friend told you the truth and cared for you in spite of it.

Somebody was knocking at the door.

John.

"Are you hungry?" I asked. "I've cooked soup …"

He didn't say anything.

I thought of my mother who had gone with a man that had come to mow the meadow behind our house. And I thought of Father who drank so much after Mother didn't come back home.

"Who are you?" I asked.

His face was bruised and scratched, a thin, handsome face.

It rained and I loved the raindrops that rolled on his cheeks. The rain had made the nameless river as big as the wind. It would give it deep pools.

"You are a thief," John said.

"Yes," I said.

"I know," he said his words as soft as breadcrumbs.

His wild hair was wet. He looked so thin in his frazzled shirt.

"I'm the one the thieves steal from," he said. "Thank you for the soup," his smile was a quiet sunset. "I have to go, Jane. There are other thieves in the world who are waiting to steal all I have from me."

He touched my hand.

"I've never met a thief like you," he said. I liked his voice. "The soup was magnificent."

He stood up and walked to the door. He closed it, and he closed the world after him.

Then I noticed something on the table. It resembled a sponge. When I looked at it closely I knew what it was: a stone, a black one I recognized.

This is crazy, I thought, scared.

"John, hey, John! John!" I ran out of the house.

"You forgot this," I shouted waving the thing that gleamed in my hand, as light as a box of matches, as bright as the moon.

"Will you keep my soul for me?" he said. "It will feel much better with you."

I couldn't breathe. I couldn't speak.

"You are beautiful," he said. "You are my nameless river that keeps my stars in its pools for me."

I couldn't say anything. I felt like crying.

I Could Buy You a Cup of Coffee

"Will you go to Sylvia 's again?" her mother asked her more than a year ago.

"Yes," Veta said and went out.

That was how her fib-telling started and she'd kept it up ever since. There was no Sylvia. She named her loneliness Sylvia so her mother didn't worry that Veta was alone all the time. Most often she remained in the library where the air smelled of beautiful paper dust, of poems which slept between the pages, of writers, forgotten a long time ago between the thick dusty covers of the books. Veta knew them all. Her loneliness waited for her in the park, too. It was tucked down the long alley that started from Lolita café and led to the railway station. It was a very insignificant railway station where the fast trains from Sofia to Greece didn't stop, only the slow ones did, once a day. The trains rocked their wagons like dark clouds that moaned under the burden of human electricity. The alley was lined with poplar trees, their branches thick with ravens—black rivets that nailed the afternoon shut. She often walked along the narrow platform, sat on the bench on which dozens of guys had scrawled dirty words. Many "Ivan + Tanya = love", but Veta didn't read the dirty remarks and didn't calculate who plus who made love. Her loneliness was soft and quiet, there were ravens and sun in it and warm empty rails that reached the end of Bulgaria and went on to the clouds in Greece. She called her loneliness Sylvia after that thin, black-eyed girl from second grade whom she taught at school.

The girl still couldn't read. She managed to spell and utter only the short three-letter nouns, but Veta loved the fairy tales the girl made up, tossing and pulling at those short, short words. Veta told the child, "Read this." Sylvia spelled out: horse, child, moon and the horse suddenly learned to fly. After a minute, it hurtled off to the moon where a little naughty child lived in a very peculiar house. Its roof was built of sun's rays and its walls were white clouds. Veta's loneliness was a soft summer, a rainy afternoon with a small railway station, dark poplars, and ravens that knit in the clouds terrific nets of courage with their black wings.

"My mother is in Italy," the girl told her one day. "She takes care of an old woman there. My grandmother is here, in Bulgaria, and she looks after a toddler boy in Sofia. Listen, I hate the long words," Sylvia admitted. "The letters are too heavy for them and they can't run. I forget what they are up to while I spell them. That's why I can't read long words. I hate to wait for them while they linger in their places and can't move on. They have letters of stones—you can take my word for that."

"I wish I had grandchildren," Veta's mother often said. She had never married. She was a pediatrician in the small provincial hospital in Pernik and took care of the newborn babies. Many winters ago, a one-year-old girl, Veta by name, was dying from viral pneumonia. The doctor didn't go home until the toddler gradually stopped running temperature and started sipping at its milk. Before the doctor adopted the child, she called her own loneliness Sofia, after the capital of Bulgaria. After work, she went to the cinema or to theater in Sofia, or simply mooned around the streets until after dinnertime.

"Perhaps we could think of somebody ... a man you'd love to see or talk to," the pediatrician said to her daughter. "The management appointed a young neurologist in the hospital a couple of months ago. We could invite him to dinner."

Of course, they invited him to dinner but the man could stand neither the ravens nor the railway station. He adored long words that had many letters in them and couldn't run at all. His mouth transformed them into threatening diagnoses which could kill anybody. In the middle of the dinner, Veta excused herself and left her mother and the young neurologist with their beefsteaks and sauté potatoes.

"Why did you do that?" her mother asked her in the morning. "It was not polite to run away on Doctor Tomov like that. You insulted him. Well, don't repeat my mistake, please. A woman should have a child. You simply .... Listen, find somebody for several weeks. Later you can go away. You and I will take care of the little one together."

"But ...," Veta began, "no. I wouldn't like that."

"You call your loneliness Sylvia," the doctor said. "You've learned that from me. I'll ask Doctor Ivanov to dinner tomorrow. He's divorced."

"I won't be at home tomorrow in the evening," Veta said.

In the afternoons, she remained in the teachers' room with Sylvia. The two of them read fairy tales from Sylvia's ABC book or solved problems about trains and sparrows.

"Miss Toneva," Sylvia said once. "You'd better have your own child because I learned to read long words. They are no longer full of stones. I even think some of them taste of chocolate. You can teach your child when you have one. What do you think?"

"It's not that easy—"

"Yesterday your Mom came to see me at school," the girl interrupted her. "Is it true you go to that small railway station every day? Why? The fast trains don't stop there and the canteen selling chocolate wafers is never open."

"I like the poplar trees," Veta said.

"Your mom asked me to find a guy who liked poplar trees and ravens for you," the child added.

"That would be silly," Veta said. "Now let's solve the problem about the two boats on page 67."

"Listen, I know such a guy. He's very tall. I'll show him to you. Your Mom says she wants you to have friends. Look at me, I have many friends and I'm okay. Come on, I'll solve the problem about the two boats by myself. If it's too difficult, Grandma will help me. Look, is it true that you call the ravens, the station, and the poplar trees after me? You can't call a raven Sylvia, and you can't call the rails Sylvia. Call them simply "station", "rails" and "ravens". Come with me."

Sylvia, who looked small for her seven years, and her teacher started off down the alley that went to Lolita café.

"Here he is," Sylvia said and pointed at the newsstand. A very tall man stood behind the heaps of bright pictures and titles of the newspapers. The girl rushed to him and said, "Here she is. She likes ravens like you."

The man fumbled in his pockets and gave the child a candy bar.

"No, I don't want it," the girl declared. "I love her. I didn't bring her here for your candies. I don't want her to stay alone with the rails. She'd better stay with you. Never mind, you are so tall."

Veta turned around and walked away down the alley.

"Hey!"

The man left his newspapers, caught up with Veta, reached for her arm and said, "That child's been telling me you like ravens. She's been repeating this for two months now."

"I have to hurry," Veta said.

"I love the railway station where you go every day. I've seen you there."

"I haven't seen you," Veta said.

"Sylvia offered to give me her box of crayons if I asked you out on a date. She said, 'You are very tall, but she'll like you all the same.' She also said you knew words that could fly."

Veta was about to leave when the newsagent added, "I want you to know that I need a box of crayons ... badly."

She turned around and looked at him, not knowing what to say. The sky was thick with spring winds and the river flowed quietly not far away from the road.

"I wonder if I could buy you a cup of coffee this evening," the man went on. "If you are busy, I can wait."

His face waited. The winds and the spring waited, too.

Veta smiled. She didn't know why.

The Drawer of My Desk

I'd like to tell you about Gallantine. I knew he was waiting for me, exhibiting his athletic body—male athletic bodies are priority number one with my mother—on the divan my father had fetched from Italy. I supposed Gall would produce convincing arguments as to how sharp my wit was, how rich and colorful an imagination God had blessed me with, and how well I spoke English. I could only surmise that the attractive blond lady who constantly hovered around Gallantine and made it known far and wide she studied pedagogy, had probably written the text which Gallantine would use to declare how impatiently he wanted me to become his wedded wife. Well, her name was Veronica, the queen of pedagogic research.

Although I possessed the weight of a combat armored vehicle, I was well capable of getting on the nerves of little fluffy kittens like Gallantine. I had made him wait for me on that divan fifty minutes now, and I hoped his handsome face was crushed like a doormat under the burden of his wounded pride. Who the hell dared make fun of him? I did, I, the fat heiress. He had perspired profusely, this was inevitable, and the smell of his first-class sweat ruined the aroma of the deodorant liquid in which Gallantine swam every day.

It was a must with me that men had to be coerced into realizing how precious I was, so I intended to keep Gall on that divan an hour more. That was a trick I had learned from my deceased father, "A guy waiting in front of your door is a chunk of stale bread, my girl. A dog wouldn't sniff at it." The thought of Gallantine as stale bread breathed new life into me.

Somebody knocked at the door. It would be more precise to say kicked at the door as if he intended to wrench it out of its fixture and that, strictly speaking, was supreme arrogance. I would not allow a chunk of stale bread to ruin the property my father had bought at the price of his own blood. An anonymous bullet assisted Dad in successfully meeting his maker. My gentleman caller knocked repeatedly at the door made of yew wood my father had delivered from

Belgium. I sent a maid to inform Gallantine I was not ready to see him. Then Mother rang me up and spoke to me in a very concerned manner.

"Gall is coming to pop the question, dear," she sighed on the telephone. "Please, be friendly with him. You know how much that man loves you."

That man ardently loved all heiresses in town; he was a lawyer whose clients drove cars, which were more expensive than the overall financial resources of our municipality. Gallantine had chosen me. That fact, apart from being an open acknowledgment of my father's money, was a topic that gave rise to unsavory comments about me.

I switched on my computer, riveted my heavenly eyes on the monitor, and called out, "Come in!"

"Good afternoon, my dear." I was right, his mouth did look like a worn-out doormat. "You look swell today. Has your mother informed you what I intend to do?"

"Yes, she has," I assured him, waiting for additional information.

"You are very beautiful," my prospective husband ventured and the doormat in his mouth cleaned my old sandals. It was obvious he wanted to appeal to me.

"I assumed you'd start with the assumption how intelligent I am," I interrupted him discreetly. "The intelligence of a human being is invisible. You can use that and be on the safe side."

"But you are really very beautiful." My fiancé had evidently let his imagination run loose. "Your eyes are green like ..." the comparison was too cumbersome to make and, willing to eliminate the awkward pause in the conversation, Gallantine pushed his lips into my mouth. In other words, he kissed me, as a proper loving husband would positively do. "You are an exceptionally intelligent woman, and I really want you to be my wife."

He produced the same sentence several months ago as he tangoed around the excessive curves of my body at my mother's party. His offer did not surprise me at all. I was interested, however, in how much he would want in return for his self-sacrifice.

"You are a person of rich and compassionate soul—"

"My soul is another good topic of discussion," I encouraged him. "It is invisible to the naked eye."

"I am serious, and I enjoy your sense of humor, too."

"Let's drop the unnecessary procedures," my voice sounded dry like the sands of the Sahara. "Despite all your admiration for my soul, my sense of humor, my rich and colorful imagination, let us concentrate on my considerable weight."

"You are so pretty," my future husband repeated stubbornly. Gallantine lacked both inspiration and imagination, and reiterated, "You are so pretty."

I remembered a scrawny Gypsy lad who had used some very similar words. Suddenly, I longed to be with that lean gypsy. He, the poor soul, frittered away all the money I had paid him on those nasty sausages. I loved him. "Yes. Yes, you really are quite ... how shall I put it ... bosomy. Yes. You are fat. And fat is fat. Well, you know it's important to get on with one's marriage partner from the spiritual point of view. To understand one's partner spiritually, one needs money."

"Gallantine," I said. "How much money do you need to understand me spiritually after you become my husband?"

"You are intelligent, I grant you that. And I appreciate the fact you speak to the point, no prejudice, no beating about the bush."

"Yes," I whispered changing the approach to our conversation. "You know what? I really thank you very much. You are such an attractive man and I am such a ... fatty." The clouds in the sky witnessed my humiliation. They knew I preferred gulping down the toads in all swamps of Bulgaria to uttering abject words about me. Well, my father used to say, "Let the brassy idiot clamber atop your head, my girl. Leave him there for a minute to check how deep into your brain he'll try to spit. Then squash him in the mud under your boots."

"Yes, you are fat," Gallantine agreed, the weighing machine in his eyes measuring the tonnage of my buttocks. "Yes, you are. You are positively familiar with the fact that your mother approves of me." Yes, I knew she approved of him on Tuesdays and Fridays in the afternoon after she had had her lunch and the beautician had refreshed her face with pineapple juice. Gallantine, however, decided to explain to me what that exactly meant. "Your Mom's great. You will become my wife. You will be Mrs. Taleva. Can you imagine it? There will be only one Mrs. Taleva in the whole country. You will be that lady. But as you know very well, everything in the world has a price," he dropped the bait of his sentence and let it hang in the air as he inserted its sharp hook into my stomach.

I had to keep my mouth shut and my eyes glued to the parquet floor. If I looked at this hamster, his poor ass would burst into flames. Even Gallantine would sense I was about to shoot him dead.

"Of course, the price is high," the hamster produced the end of his statement. "Forty percent of your father's property, my dear, and you will become Mrs. Taleva in return. If you interpret this sentence from the standpoint of diplomacy, it means that you'll be welcome to all drawing rooms of the elite, although I find it hard to imagine what you'll talk to these people about. Perhaps you'll have to read some books on art or on law. I have built my reputation painstakingly for so many years now. You'll be invited to all major receptions, and you'll have at your disposal—"

"Forty percent is too high a price," I blurted out, then I swallowed my rage and shut up.

"Apart from your sojourns in the elite houses of the capital, I will be in your bed once a month on a regular basis," Gallantine assured me. It was evident he was not overjoyed to take this opportunity. "Perhaps you'll get pregnant although I strongly doubt it."

If my father had heard about the young snail's plans, he would have crushed his shell.

"Thank you," I whispered carefully pulling open the drawer of my desk. "Probably the rest of the month you'll share my mother's company or that of the blond lady you study pedagogy with."

"Yes, you are quite right, dear. An honest man should not live in loneliness, don't you think? You and I can often talk on the telephone— for example, Mondays in the morning. Let me sum it up: forty percent, and let us decide on the date of our official wedding ceremony. If you conceive a child by me, dear, all doors of legal entities and institutions will be open for him. I personally will introduce him to a number of eminent families. His photographs will be in all newspapers. As for you, you are his mother."

"Perhaps all that deserves fifty percent of my father's property," I whispered. Anger burned a tunnel into my brain, but a fat young woman like me should never drive the sledge of anger. "What will you say about sixty percent?" I purred, sticking my eyes into my belly button. I had no desire to look at him.

"You know what? You are very fat, but you're cool," the hamster smiled encouragingly making a pass at me. "Sixty is my favorite number."

"I don't need money," I lied brazenly. "All I need is your love. If I make it sixty-five percent will you visit my bed twice a month?"

Gallantine's face lit up inspired by the vision of our bright future.

"You are very cool. Very cool indeed," he whispered. "If you want we can make love here and now!"

I had already managed to open the desk drawer, so I thrust my fat hand into it and dragged out a Makarov pistol. Makarov is a good gun, and I hope my father had made proper use of it before his competitors sent him to the world beyond. I lifted Makarov's muzzle to Gallantine's mouth, although the man had already planted his hand in the glen between my breasts.

"What about eighty percent?" I asked pressing Makarov against his forehead. My future husband choked as he gulped the air under his nose.

"Get ... th ... this gun aa ... way!" he stammered, chopping the words with the red saw of his tongue. "G-g-get it away!"

I hit his nose with the handle of the pistol. "Would you like eighty-five percent?" I repeated the question in a pleasant tone of voice. Perspiration ran down his smooth forehead. "I am a very good shot," I lied. "This piece of iron has a silencer."

My future husband grabbed at his stomach with both hands, ready to throw up any minute now, a big blond pile of legal knowledge stewing in his own juice. He had probably wet his high-quality pants.

"Tomorrow you will introduce me to the eminent families in the capital of Bulgaria, and I will prepare your business program for the week." He pressed his stomach with both hands and was on the verge of puking on the parquet floor my father had delivered from Spain.

"D-d-don't sh-shoot!"

"The day after tomorrow, December 20th, you and I will pay a visit to Mr. and Mrs. Anev." The hamster groped for his heart. He had a sore throat, no doubt about that, for he tried hard to spit something out of his foaming mouth.

"Yes-y-yess, dear."

"Otherwise you'll acquire an exceptionally interesting part of my father's property, a nice leaden bullet in the medulla oblongata. I hope it makes exactly seventy-five percent of my father's assets, doesn't it?"

I was afraid that Gallantine was unable to calculate the exact percentage just now. The doormat on his face cleaned my slippers and Gall, the most prestigious catch at parties trembled and shook like an aspen leaf.

"Dear," I croaked using all my compassion. "If someone learns how you asked me to become your wife—a proposal, which I have already accepted—I will make sure you won't survive to attend the next meeting of the lawyers' league. Do I make myself clear?" I pressed my father's Makarov harder against my future husband's forehead and got no reply, alas. That induced me to force a part of the muzzle between Gallantine's crimson lips." Well, will you love me loyally and with all your heart 'til death do us part?"

It is difficult for a human being to speak with a muzzle of a gun between his or her teeth, but Gallantine coped with this impossible situation.

"Yes, I will love you," his words did not sound sad although I saw tears in his eyes.

I was happy. My holiday season began.

The Last Night's Excitement

Basil had decided to let himself go … all the way. He had spent last night with a blonde again and had not even bothered to remember her name. She had told him she had died and been regenerated seven times, and Basil had pretended to believe her, but the superficial black stripes on her shoulders and head, when you parted her hair, told a different story. Especially the ones on her head. They were so close together they gave him chills up and down his spine. She must have been in the regenerating rooms at least a dozen times, probably in the "deluxe" accommodations, the treatment followed by a lavish and costly procedure—the color of her skin summoned thoughts of fabulously expensive balm. Basil had erased her face from his videotheque, but he was still in the throes of last night's excitement, so he decided to indulge himself with another blonde tonight. He knew that pleasures of this sort cost approximately three times his salary, but he was sure he would fail the physical exam this month and then would be forced into the standard regenerating rooms. The treatment left such deep and visible dark gray lines all over the body that afterward one looked like a quilt sewn together from differently colored rags and bits of fabric. He considered himself born under a lucky star because the computer for initiating intimate contacts had paired him with such a charming creature—flaxen-haired, with green eyes that moved about in a distracted way, and an appearance that, at first glance, revealed no signs of her ever having set foot in a standard regenerating room. Impatient, Basil wanted to proceed to the dark hotel room for which he had paid a fat bundle. But when the woman said a few words, he felt goose-bumps up and down his back and slowed his steps.

"You know, death looks quite becoming on you, dummy. Don't try to fight it! Don't try to hide the lines on your skin! They give a fierce expression to your face. You know, I sometimes envy those who go through the standard procedure."

Basil hesitated. He could get rid of her—the woman was obviously crazy. But after a moment's thought, he remembered that the computer for initiating intimate contacts had already charged him for the room, so he decided against it. The blonde woman had already started to caress him and that switched on a pleasant sensation. Crazy or not, at least she does it well, he thought. Besides, I'll never see her again. Actually, the rules for intimate contacts did allow partners to meet repeatedly, but no one ever did. It would have been much too boring. The woman went on with her chatter.

"Just imagine, dummy. Sometimes I spend six months without having to use the regenerating rooms"

Though he was generally regarded as a stable, well-composed person who could control himself, Basil trembled visibly. This one was definitely off her rocker, not that all the ones he had met before had been sane. Actually, Seva, the only woman whose name he could remember and about whom he kept inquiring among his colleagues, was also mad. So mad, in fact, that he couldn't think about her without ending up dead drunk, thus using up his next two or three paychecks before he had even received them. Seva—an unusual name. When he had heard it for the first time he had made fun of it. He knew he would never see her again.

"Six months and not a single viral infection in my blood! No rheumatism, no diabetes, nothing. I'm completely healthy."

Basil decided to ignore her rambling and babbling. He knew for a fact that it was impossible to survive on the earth for more than a month without resorting to the regenerating rooms. The atmosphere was so filled with poisons and toxins that your lungs fell apart in forty days. Contact with the soil turned your skin into dust within a week. Water discolored and decomposed your blood in a month or so, provided you drank it in small doses. At least that's what he had been told; he himself had never stayed away from the regenerating room for more than fifteen days.

"Six months without regeneration!" He grunted, trying to humor her. "Where do you work, honey?"

"At the Resurrection Laboratory," she chimed in. "Everything there is so sterile, so boring, that—"

Basil whistled. "The Resurrection laboratory!" Some of the people who worked there could be quite refined, but sometimes they felt drawn to brutal, primitive characters, and put their numbers in a regular computer for initiating intimate contacts. But who cared? People got tired of always being among the elite. Basil had chanced upon just such a woman. Maybe he could ask her. He was wary. Still, he could ask, but it was too soon. Perhaps a little later. Basil swore under his breath. The week after they dragged Seva away in a police van he and two colleagues had tried to die permanently. Naturally, they had been regenerated once more and sent back to work. Society needed their golden hands, their invaluable experience — that's what the television commentator had said.

Basil had even received a pay-raise. Still, he had little tolerance for this society, this horde of dreary characters who had been regenerated a million times. Sometimes he wished he would never be resurrected again, would never have to go back to his dingy office and dreary job as a wholesale distributor of soap and cosmetics. But there was nothing he could do about it. It was much cheaper to regenerate the sickly and diseased and let them loose on the hazards of life fit and healthy than it was to purify the sludge-like soil or the brownish muck they called water by force of habit. The need to have children born had disappeared and so had the need to squander money on hospitals, schools, kindergartens and nursery schools. People came back regenerated, their experience intact, their health fully restored, bragging about this disease or that they had had earlier but had been cured of and so on until the next dying time. Women didn't lose their sexual savvy — like this doll here. She was okay. Real death simply ceased to exist. And yet Basil hated his job as a wholesale soap distributor with a passion.

"You know, dummy", blurted the blonde excitedly, "once they nearly threw me out of the Laboratory. Do you know why?"

"Why?" Basil echoed listlessly.

"I absentmindedly left a patient's blood plasma out in the sun. You have no idea what happened to this man after we regenerated him. The poor idiot had a horn growing right out of his chest! He went berserk. He gutted the chief surgeon, ripped open the faces of a couple of nurses ... What excitement! Naturally, we had to regenerate all of them.

Basil felt himself getting tense. He licked his lips with a gravelly tongue. His blood pounded away in his temples.

"And whatever happened to that character, the one with the horn?"

"We had to liquidate him, of course," laughed the blonde.

"And then you ran him through the regenerators again?"

"Absolutely not! We liquidated him forever."

Basil let out a groan. The blonde kissed him and resumed her benumbing prattle. But he was thinking of Seva—that mad woman. "I want a child" she had said to Basil. "A real child. Mine and yours. I'll take care of it. Please, hide me somewhere. At your office."

At first, Basil had said no. Then he thought, Why not? He took Seva to his squalid hole of a place. At least that way they wouldn't withhold money from his sex account until the police inspectors found her. And then the child was born. Basil thought he would kill it himself; he had never heard of a child being born and couldn't even start guessing what kind of fine they'd impose on him for it. He had hidden Seva and taken her through the regenerating rooms illegally. This was going to cost him a fine of a quarter of a million. He had to get rid both of Seva and the baby. But he couldn't do it; from the moment the boy was born everything had changed. He would hurry like mad to get home. He would lean over his old clothes where the little one lay cuddled. He would pay outrageous sums of money for clean, filtered water. Eventually, however, the police found Seva. Basil couldn't find out who had betrayed him; probably some friend who sincerely felt for him and wanted to spare him the disgrace and the huge fine.

"My colleagues will never believe I ever came into contact with a person like you," said Basil. The blonde laughed.

"Take this," she said, thrusting a bundle of cash into his hand. "Now they will believe you."

"The word was going around that you had regenerated some baby in your laboratory," Basil ventured. The blonde tensed up nervously in his grasp, so he added quickly, "Maybe we shouldn't talk of such things?"

"No, we shouldn't," the woman smiled, calming down. "Apparently, some perverse character had wanted something stupid like that around. The woman with the baby refused to give his name."

Seva! It dawned on him like a huge submarine suddenly emerging from the depths of the ocean. Seva. She had not betrayed him. Of course, she hadn't. If she had told on him they would've sent him to Seycard. There, the regenerating rooms were set up so that when you came out your eyes popped out and glazed over, and you went mute. But there is even a use for idiots. Doctors must have material to experiment on, after all. So Seva had not betrayed him. Mad, stark raving mad. She could have accused him of rape and coercion, but she hadn't. He had promised his annual salary as a reward for any information on her. Maybe someone had run into her in some intimate contact. Yet no one had ever responded. He was going crazy with fear that they had sent her to Seycard, so he signed on as a volunteer to go and repair the facilities there, but he didn't find her. The thought of her being with someone else drove him insane with jealousy. But at least that was preferable to knowing with certainty that they had not regenerated her, that she had disappeared from the face of the earth. "Seva. My dear ..."

"What?" the blonde shrieked in delight. "My dear? Is that what you just called me? You're incredible sweetie."

"Dear?" Where had he picked up the word? No one had used it in years. Seva. Seva. Seva.

"Did you really regenerate that baby?" Basil threw in gingerly.

"Why in the world would we do that? No, we left it to its own end."

"To its end? To ... die?" he froze with fear at the sound of the word. "To die forever?"

"Of course, dummy." The blonde woman smiled and started stroking his hair. "Both the baby and his hare-brained mother, who, come to think of it, wasn't bad looking at all. Will anybody believe that you called me "My dear?" I really liked it, though it did sound kind of loony, didn't it?"

If only he had tried to stop the paramedics when they took the baby away. Basil hadn't shown his face at all. That would have meant regeneration at Seycard for sure. He remembered how the day before he had taken the little one's fingers and put them to his own cheek. Loony, true, but nice. It had felt so nice. Somehow, he had hoped that at some point in his life he would see a boy and say to himself, That's my boy. He had hoped, but they'd see. He'd show them. Maybe it would have been better if Seva had betrayed him back then.

"They'll see, all of them," he kept repeating after the blonde beauty had departed. His joints hurt, his heart had been rattling irregularly for quite some time. He was definitely due for another regeneration. As usual, Basil prepared his blood plasma carefully. But this time, contrary to all instructions, he left the transparent container out in the sun for more than an hour. "They'll see, Seva." Basil hated his job at the soap office more than ever before.

His first impulse when he emerged from the next dying and regeneration routine was to reach out and feel his chest "Seva, my dear," he whispered. Those forgotten, silly words. In the middle of his chest cavity, his shaking fingers touched a crusty, sharp-edged protrusion.

It was a huge, heavy horn.

They didn't know!

Choking on Air

"Some are very mean," Old Julian said. "They stay in your bones. You wail like a wolf at the moon and you don't know where you are. You look for the same one after you've drunk the whole bottle. She remains in your bones and gives you headaches."

"One can't trust the bottling companies," his friend Pete muttered. "These companies thrust all sorts of impurities in that water. You pay through the nose for nothing."

It was at that point that Pete noticed I was listening to what he was grumbling.

"Mary, mind your business," Pete said. He'd never liked me. I was the new waitress in the *Jar Girls* and on the very first day he set his eyes on me, he shouted, "Bring me a red one and get out of my way!"

He had a nasty way of patting the table with his hand. They'd told me where the red ones were—the bottles of water into which the red-haired girls had been dissolved. Old Julian had ordered me to store the red ones in the biggest pantry. The red ones were the most expensive of all. There were black ones and blonde ones, too. Old Julian said there was no way an ordinary guy could check what he was buying, a redhead or a black one.

The color of the hair made no difference if you asked me. The read ones were simply very expensive and Old Julian made me say any bottle of water had a redhead dissolved in it.

Pete once blabbed out the red ones tasted differently. They were bittersweet and were very quick, quick in the sense that the buyers didn't have to wait long for their pleasure.

Pete hated my guts for no reason at all. He made me drink a red one once. He gave me a hundred-dollar bill before I had even brought the bottle with the red one from the cellar. I should have suspected the mean trick he was going to pull on me. I drank half of the bottle. Old Julian later told me he caught me the moment before I pulled the trigger, trying to put a bullet through my brain.

"What did you see?" he asked me. "Why did you want to kill yourself?"

"I tell you if you tell me what was in that bottle Pete made me drink," I mumbled.

In the very beginning, I didn't know that Old Julian and Pete dissolved girls in that special water. I knew nothing about the money they offered you to dissolve as much as your finger in it.

Old Julian told me once he stumbled upon that spring in his backyard by chance. He told me he was looking for his dog when he noticed a hole in the narrow patch of land behind his shack. It was in July, he said, a day hotter than hell, and he had neither whiskey nor water at home.

One called July half of the time on Dobra, the little unholy hole, which was used as a prison. The Hole's population consisted mostly of criminals; the Hole was so far away from the rest of the world, and the rumors about it were its best guard. Old Julian, who had probably killed somebody, otherwise he wouldn't have been here, found out that his dog had fallen into that mineral in his backyard. He didn't know there was a spring in the first place. The sky in July was mighty green and the stones loomed green, too. If it had been December, it would've been even worse, Old Julian told me.

December was colder than the freezer in the central station where the cops threw you to cool out if you were about to die or suffocate in the green dust of the wilderness. Old Julian heard his dog Blackie wailing like hell and then suddenly there was silence. Julian saw what happened to his Blackie: the dog dissolved for a split second and was no more. But it was July, old Julian said his voice heavy with guilt. He had neither whiskey nor water so he crawled to the hole and started lapping the water into which his Blackie had vanished.

"You wouldn't believe it, Mary," he said. "It felt like Blackie was with me, on his mat under the window. It felt like Blackie licking my hands. That's what I liked most about Blackie, his licking my hands. That water from the hole in my backyard gave me my Blackie back. I could hear him padding after me and I could hear him bark."

Of course, it was Pete who had an idea, Old Julian told me.

"What if we dissolved a girl in that water in your backyard, Julian?"

There were not so many girls in the Hole anyway, but Pete had a girlfriend at the time, Frieda by name.

At first, no one wanted to drink the water with Frieda in it. But one guy finally tried it. On the following day, the same guy came back again, thrust his head into the muddy puddle in the Old Julian's backyard and guzzled and swigged and spluttered. Pete could hardly wrench him away from the tiny patch of water. After that the guy groaned and moaned, sighed and shouted, "Frieda, Frieda, Frieda." His face looked as happy as if he had that Frieda all over the place. Then another guy came and had a bottle of Frieda.

With time, there was less and less of Frieda in the water gushing forth from the spring in the backyard. By that time, Pete had another girlfriend, Carla. At a certain point, the guys who drank the water from that hole moaned and groaned, whispered and shouted, "Carla. Carla."

Then other guys shouted, "Elizabeth, Elizabeth!"

Of course, Old Julian's shack disappeared and a new, rich and clean house took its place by the hole with the water. Julian founded "True Love Ltd" and Pete founded a bottling company. The two of them opened a pub, Jar Girls, in which they sold that water.

They wallowed in money. The criminals who had been deported to the Hole queued in front of the Jar Girls no matter if it was July or December. All the time there were men sprawling on the sidewalk near the pub, wailing, "Clara," or "Jane," or "Beth." Pete paid me to collect them, to wash them and drag them to the dormitory, which was initially meant to be a warehouse for the bottles of the redheads.

Jar Girls was a great pub. Men didn't drink whiskey or brandy here. They drank redheads, blond heads, and very rarely a black head. To tell you the truth, I'd rather collect a drunken man than a man blubbering "Clara" or "Beth". The ones who'd had a redhead cursed me, kicked me, and clawed at my hair. They wanted their Beth, or their Patricia, or their Dora. Sprawling bodies and drooling faces in front or behind the pub didn't work for the good image of the enterprise. In July, the heat killed a couple of fellows who were too heavy for me to drag to the dormitory.

It was easier for me in December, the clients drank their redheads in the dormitory, and I had to clean the debris they scattered in their wake, but I didn't mind the mess. The dormitory was constantly reverberating with deep groans and wails. All the beds in it were occupied. There were shaky and rusty frames with tattered mattresses on them, but the men who had drunk a redhead paid the price of a luxury hotel room for their greasy mattresses under the roof. December colds were notorious in the Hole. The best pastime in December was a bottle of Pete's water.

"They give you big tips," Pete said. He meant the drunken guys I dragged to the dormitory. That was a lie of course. The men never saw me. They saw their redheads. When they drank *that water*, they didn't notice anybody around them. They were blissfully happy with the girl in their bottle.

I knew what they saw and I knew how they felt. I had a redhead myself. In fact, that redhead had black hair. She told me she loved me more than the air she breathed and more than the earth she walked on. She said she was fed up with the drunkards I had to clean for. Pete made me drink a bottle of that black-haired girl. Old Julian had difficulty in wrenching the pistol from my hands.

"You should have let her kill herself," I heard Pete mumbling to Old Julian. "She's a busybody and she *is* a bitch. I don't like her at all."

Old Julian said nothing.

"Mary," Old Julian said after Pete splashed a can of beer on my face to make me come to my senses, he wanted me to get down to scraping the floor of the dorm as soon as possible. "Mary, I've got something important to tell you. I don't want you to answer me right away."

"What is, Julian? You want to fire me?"

"Look at the grass," he said.

The grass was as red as ever. No one looked at the grass in the Hole. In July, the grass was ambers and set fire to your shoes and, if you touched it in December, you saw things that were not there.

"Why should I look at the grass, Julian?" I asked him. He was a rich man now and the spring with that water was still in his backyard.

"You know what?" he drawled. "Yesterday I sprinkled some of the special water on the grass, Mary."

He paused, his black eyes on my face.

"You couldn't imagine what happened," he went on.

"If you want to fire me, Julian, there is no use speaking about the damned grass."

"After I sprinkled some of that water on the grass the spring in my backyard went dry."

I looked at his face—it was big and beefy; his eyes were bleary. I wondered what crime he had committed before the cops threw him into the Hole.

"Julian, there is water in the spring in the backyard," I said. "I saw it an hour ago. The spring hasn't run dry."

He squinted at me.

"Mary, I think Pete has forbidden you to hang around the spring," Old Julian drawled. "How come you know there's water in there?"

I never knew where I was with Julian. There were moments I suspected he kind of liked me, yet I didn't know why they had deported him in the Hole.

"I wanted to make an experiment," I said.

"An experiment?" he breathed. "What experiment?"

"I stole a glass of your water."

"I know," he said and snickered. "I saw you trying to dissolve your finger in the glass. Did you want to give the water to some guy to drink? Did you really hope the bloke would marry you?" Julian laughed harshly.

"No," I said. "I wanted to dissolve a man in the water and I wanted to drink it. I feel very lonely here with all these slobbering idiots."

He looked at me, his eyes sharp and cold.

"You wouldn't do that," he rasped.

It was July, and there were no nights in July. We called it nighttime when the grass turned blue. Then the blades were not embers. If you stepped on the grass your skin itched. After the itching stopped, it was different with different people. Some hit their heads with their fists, others were very quiet. That was a bad sign. The quiet ones went far deep into the grass wasteland and didn't come back.

"Pete said to me something happened to you when he sprinkled some of the special water on the grass," Julian said staring at me. "Something happened and it was odd." His breath was on my face and I could feel the acrid smell of the water with a redhead in it.

"You've been drinking," I said.

"I've had a drink," he grumbled. "Isn't it strange I don't groan and I don't wail?"

"You are a strange man," I said taking a step back from his beefy face.

"Well, I made an experiment, too," he said squinting at me. "I dipped your finger in the special water while you were asleep."

My hands shook.

"They look fine, your fingers, don't they?" he whispered. "I wanted to dissolve your forefinger and your thumb."

"You doped me, eh?" I barked. "You doped me so I couldn't feel anything. You tried to dissolve my fingers! It's worse than rape."

"I doped you all right," he agreed. "But look at your hands now. Your forefinger and thumb should be missing."

"You've drunk too much of that redhead," I said. "You are imagining things." His sharp eyes were on my face but I was not afraid of his stare. I looked him in the eye as I shrieked, "You smoked dried December grass and you imagined you did things you hadn't done."

"I and Pete sprinkled some water on the grass and the spring went dry," Old Julian said.

"There's water in your spring now," I objected. "I was there and I saw it."

Julian didn't seem to hear me.

"Pete said that when the spring went dry he noticed something happened to you." He grabbed my hand and squeezed it hard. "Pete said that he saw your face. It was as blue as the grass. He said your skin glowed."

"Pete has never liked me," I said.

There was no wind and the air was thick with the heat of July. The grass was blue which meant that the night had come.

"Edith, queer things happen to you," Julian said under his breath. "I dissolve your fingers and they are back in place, your face glows like the grass, the water in the spring disappears ...."

"You've been smoking from the dried December grass," I said.

"Who are you, Edith? I drank from the water into which I dissolved you. It is not the same like it was with Frieda."

The grass was blue now, deep intense blue that somehow made the heat bearable. I liked the grass and I wasn't afraid of it. The guys who didn't have money for a glass of redhead dried it and smoked it, others, the most impatient ones, simply chewed the blades raw. Those guys that went to pick more grass vanished and the wasteland became thicker and more intensely blue. Nobody cared about a guy who smoked the blue grass. Nobody cared about a guy who didn't smoke.

"We made a little experiment with you, I and Pete," Old Julian said. "It was a very curious experiment."

He produced a gun, but I wasn't afraid. I had got accustomed to men brandishing guns under my nose. Guns were useless when men groaned, "Frieda, Frieda," sticking out their tongues at the white wind trying to cool off. The more prudent ones gave me their guns before they drank their redhead. Many shot their brains out for no reason at all. Perhaps their Frieda didn't want them.

"You aren't afraid of my gun," Julian said.

"No," I answered.

"Strange," Julian whispered. "When we made you drink the redhead you didn't try to put a bullet through your brain."

"Oh, didn't I?" I said watching his face. It was big, fat and greasy. The muzzle of his gun pressed my forehead.

"Pete and I threw you into that water, in the spring."

His hand trembled a little. When men had had too much of that water they shook for hours, especially in July when the heat made them itchy.

"You didn't dissolve into the water, Mary," Julian said. "The spring didn't run dry and you were in it, grinning."

"You've been drinking too much of these redheads," I told him. "You're not young anymore and that water might be dangerous for you."

"Then Pete shot you. You didn't die. You stood up, grinning."

"Now I'm sure you've been chewing the blue grass without cooking it first," I told him. "The clients at the bar told you not to do that."

"Then Pete vanished. I shot you, too, "old Julian said. "You just stood there, grinning."

"Oh, did I?"

"Who are you, Mary?"

It was quiet, nothing stirred. There was a time when I enjoyed silence. Now it was nothing to me.

"I'm the air you breathe in," I told him.

"What?" he gasped.

"You breathed me and you became worse, meaner, and crueler. I let you have that special water. And you killed your women in it."

"What are you talking about?" he shouted. Then he shot at me. The sound felt like the dry blue grass cracking under one's feet. I liked that sound, it was like the wind, and what was the wind? There was wind when the air was in love.

"Did you kill Pete?" old Julian breathed.

"The air doesn't kill," I said. "The air simply was not there for Pete to breathe in."

"Is he dead?"

"The air never kills. Especially old and tired air like me," I said. "Pete is a winter day."

"What?" Old Julian shouted. "You are crazy, you idiot."

"Pete is a winter day, cold and lonely," I said. "He will come back in December."

The blue grass glowed and I loved its warm inviting color. I looked at Julian's big face and I wondered why he wasn't afraid. I remembered how sad he was after his dog had died in the mineral spring.

"I wonder if it's fun to be a winter day," Julian said.

I liked the way Julian spoke about his dog. I was amazed how he grieved for Frieda, the first redhead who fell into that water.

"Listen, Julian," I tried to explain. "If I wanted, you all would be winter days in a matter of seconds. But I was curious, Julian." Yes, I was curious. The air needed wind, and each man was a breeze, a freezing cold or a scorching hot one.

"You're lying to me. You can't be air!" Julian said.

I laughed. He could make me laugh, that beefy-faced man. The blue grass glowed in the heat.

"Maybe you'll be my July wind after you die, Julian," I said, looking at him. "We have to try."

The Forbidden Trio

I didn't know why she'd taken to me. She was old, she had a bad limp, and her cheeks were wrinkled. Looking at her face made me think of the river that had run dry in the narrow sand valley; her eyes were deep dangerous crevices between wind-bitten dunes. I saw her sluggishly cross the stream, her old feet trembling, her stick creaking under her weight.

One day, my dog Sparky followed her. The minute his paw touched the water in the stream, he turned into a cloud of dust. No one knew why the stream didn't run dry and why the water in it was green. It flowed monotonously, quietly, and behind it, the hill, dark and sharp, towered over the drab shacks of the village. The old woman was the only one who waded across the greenish mud and the only one she talked to was me. Every time she glanced at me, I saw an unsettling gleam in her eyes.

I didn't know what was so interesting about me. There used to be four of us, strong and perfectly trained. Our task was to climb the hill that jutted out like a bad tooth in the brown valley. We had to study it. Studying the hill meant finding answers to a number of questions like how come that old woman managed to splash through the stream and get to the other side? She didn't turn into dust.

Another problematic issue: that little girl Peta. The child crawled over to the green stream and wallowed in it. A funny thing happened. Mrs. Jackson, Peta's mother, hinted at it first, but we thought the woman was too drunk and she was just telling us one of her tall tales.

"Peta screamed her head off while she tumbled about in the stream," Mrs. Jackson said. Even I didn't know what the woman's first name was. "Every time Peta screams we're in for trouble. I guess someone will die." Mrs. Jackson's tone of voice was flat and indifferent.

Shortly before noon, my roommate John, the most handsome and the most impatient among us, followed the little girl to the stream. I hated thinking of what happened to him. He turned into a little mound of dust that slowly settled in front of his own hut. I couldn't remember whose idea it was, maybe it was mine. What if we threw a stone into the green mud in the shallows or a piece of firewood? Simon, my best friend, chose a pebble, a small, flat one, and chucked it into the water. The dust my best friend turned into vanished without a trace, but I sensed weightless specks descend on my skin. A minute after that deep wounds gaped open on my cheeks. Peta, the little girl, stared at my disfigured face as she squatted in front of me. The little one had green eyes, too, dangerously dark green like the whirlpool that didn't run dry.

"Go away," I said.

"I don't want you to become dust," the child said.

She smiled and went rambling near the stream. A minute later, I could swear I saw the old woman with her trembling feet and face like dry sandstone sitting by the green pool. I expected I'd see the girl there. The little one was nowhere in sight. That was weird. I couldn't explain where she'd hidden. The narrow square lay deserted, perfectly quiet before my eyes.

Another funny thing happened.

"Jake, I can get ten years younger if you want me to," Mrs. Jackson said looking me in the eye. "Just say it and I will."

"I like you the way you are," I said and that was the truth. She was an odd woman and there was no telling what she'd do.

Two of us, Boris and I, had survived the stream so far. We lived near the village and tried to establish friendly relations with the locals. It turned out that was impossible. The locals were a peculiar lot. They collected the dust our colleagues had turned into and sprinkled it on their food.

"Jake, you are friends with Mrs. Jackson, and she'll collect your dust," Boris said, winking at me.

"You are friends with her, too," I said.

Mrs. Jackson appeared to be friends with anyone who bought her booze. She was the only young woman in the damned place. Her eyes were green like a thousand springs with their green grass and leaves and all. They were bitter and dangerous like the pools in that stream that had springs in it, too.

"You're a fool, Jake," Boris said. "The woman has a crush on you. And you may be the next." You may be the next was another way of saying you'll be the next to turn into dust.

"I don't give a damn about Mrs. Jackson," I said. "She's a drunk and there's nothing more to her."

There was.

"Who takes care of your child when you get drunk?" I had asked the woman once after we had sex in her shabby living room.

"Peta's old enough to take care of herself," she said. I thought I saw a gleam in her eyes.

"Why do you drink so much?"

"It's none of your business," she snapped.

I remembered I'd asked Mrs. Jackson something I had wanted to know for a long time.

"Who's Peta's father, Mrs. Jackson?"

"She'd rather it was you," she said.

I stared.

I remembered something Boris had said.

"That Peta kid," Boris had muttered under his breath. "She follows you everywhere you go, Jake."

"I give her small glass figures to play with," I explained to him. "Glass cats, glass dogs, you know them. They cost 10 cents apiece."

Boris had a peculiar way of looking at people. His yellow eyes were cold and stinging.

"And that old woman ... she speaks only to you, Jake. Why has the vixen chosen you? Mrs. Jackson has sex with you. Peta, the sassy chit of a girl treads on your heels. Does that mean that you are different from us?" His yellow eyes were on my face and all I could say was I hated the feeling of uncertainty they gave me.

A day or two after that, the old woman came to the compound and said, clutching at her stick, "I want to have a word with Jake."

"Jake can't talk to you 'til the afternoon," Boris said. "You have to wait. I've ordered him to do something and he's busy right now."

That was a fat lie.

Boris was a peculiar sort of a guy. He'd never do anything right away, that'd make him look cheap, he thought. He was a man to be reckoned with, and the crone should be well aware of that.

"I'm not like you, Jake," he said his yellow eyes biting me. "I'm not a lackey."

A lackey: that was what he started calling me after Mrs. Jackson shouted she'd rather have lunch with me than put up with his whims and vagaries. The compound knew that if one had lunch with Mrs. Jackson he'd had sex with her.

However, days were not the same anymore. The dust our colleagues had turned into and their empty cells had changed everything for the worse.

Our compound used to be a vertical jagged crag in which we had dug our hiding-places. It was cool in them, and what rendered them even more useful was that they faced the hill. The problem was that sometimes at night the air sang. Perhaps it would be better to say the air was quite noisy above the hill. The locals lived in cabins built with stones and sticks and they didn't mind the screaming air. It had been there before their grandfathers died and it did them no harm.

In front of the compound, the old woman hit the ground with her stick.

"Hi, Tasha," I heard Mrs. Jackson say.

I hadn't noticed when she'd sneaked to the narrow flat square strewn with sharp stones. She'd been drinking again, and the air around her smelled of cheap whiskey.

"I'd like to talk to Jake," the old woman said.

"You'll be wasting your time," Mrs. Jackson scoffed. "Jake is as blind as a bat. Otherwise, he should have guessed."

"What should I have guessed?" I asked.

Mrs. Jackson didn't answer. The truth was Mrs. Jackson had asked me to her cabin more than once. I thought she was pretty and I brought her little presents. Not that I liked her that much. Not that I cared. She was so lonely her desperation crushed me. Her loneliness was in the wine she poured into a cracked glass for me, in the wind she listened to, in the sand that covered her backyard. Her days were an endless wait for someone she wanted to see, a guest that never showed up at her table. Mrs. Jackson had a glass of wine that remained in front of the empty chair, and she didn't allow me to drink it. She didn't touch that glass, either.

"I'm waiting, Jake," the old woman's calm voice sounded bringing me back to reality.

"Give her some tea, Jake," Boris said. He behaved as if he were my boss which he wasn't. His gruffness annoyed me.

"I don't have tea," I said.

The old woman's eyes were hard amidst the endless creases of her face. She was meager, almost as tall as Mrs. Jackson, and her hands looked very small as she advanced slowly towards me. I wondered what her hands reminded me of. I was sure I had seen hands like hers, but I couldn't remember where. There was something weird about her steps, too, she made no noise, and her bare feet didn't stir the dust.

"What do you want with me?" I asked her.

"You are an explorer, aren't you?" She said. Her voice was melodious like a handful of pebbles that the wind grabbed from the valley and hurled at the clouds.

"Yes, I am an explorer," I answered. "But there's nothing I can explore here. The stream will turn me into a heap of dust."

"A heap of soft dust?" She smiled and the creases of her face were as deep as the dry river that had no beginning and no end.

I liked her wrinkles and the way they made her face a part of the warm day, a part of the sun that had no beginning and no end.

"Come with me to the hill," she said. "I'll show you something."

I couldn't believe what I'd just heard.

"I'll show you what happened to your colleagues" the old woman breathed.

"They're as dead as the dry stones on the river bed," Boris said.

"Shut up," the crone said her creased face glowing hard.

Boris had survived two hills he told me once after I treated him to whiskey. To survive a hill meant he destroyed the hill before the hill destroyed him.

"I'll teach you some respect, old woman," Boris snarled. "Shall I drop that Peta brat into a whirlpool?"

"Don't touch the child," I told him.

"Is this because you shack up with her mother?" he said in a tone of voice I disliked.

It was summer. It was always summer in the compound and the heat had no beginning and no end.

"I don't want to die," Boris who had survived two hills said. His eyes mocked me. I didn't say anything. "If you want to live, you destroy the ones that cross the river and go to hide on the hill."

To survive a hill meant that the hill disappeared of its own accord, or the stream vanished and the explorer went home. One never knew how a hill would behave. A handful of maniacs like us had to explore it. The locals didn't mind the hill. They said it had been harmless for centuries. Most of the people I knew called the hill explorers *crackpots*. As a rule, *hill* explorers turned to dust. Some hills were said to turn men into precious crystals, but I believed this was sheer nonsense. A hill could turn a man into a madman, yes. That had happened before. Explorers were forbidden to desert from a hill.

"Tomorrow's my last chance to take you to the hill, Jake," the old woman said, her green eyes cold and distant. "You wasted your chance today."

She hit the ground with her stick and walked away making no noise, stirring no dust, trudging the path to the hill.

The hill wanted us dead was what I thought.
That night Mrs. Jackson and I got drunk together. I'd never drunk so heavily in my life, and Mrs. Jackson had never seemed so beautiful to me. There was that third glass on the table she didn't let me touch.

"It's for Peta's father," she said. "And he was a good man."

It was the first time she had spoken about him. Her voice was dry and even.

"Peta's father was a drunk, of course. One day he said he'd go buy bread. He brought no bread and didn't return. He went to the hill." She stopped mumbling and I thought she'd fallen asleep. But she hadn't.

"I loved Peta's father," Mrs. Jackson said. "I miss him. You are worse than his old shoes." Suddenly her voice was sharp. "Your dead colleagues were a bunch of idiots. At least you drink."

I was curious what would happen next.

I had already made up my mind to follow the old woman to the hill. I had asked her how it felt to turn into a cloud of dust. You'll see, she'd said. I felt no fear and that was strange. Peta didn't scream that night.

In the morning, Boris said, "You'll be a dead man if you go with the old bitch. I don't like you, Jake. I don't mind if you kick the bucket, but I'd hate to be the only explorer in these parts."

On the following day, the old woman knocked at my door. Her wrinkled face was like a dune at sunset, all its wrinkles smiling at me, her hard green eyes watching me closely.

"Are you ready?" she asked.

Boris ran to us panting.

"He's not coming," he hissed.

"He is," she snapped, not bothering to look up.

Boris was about to say something but she waved her hand and turned her back to him. Then she looked at me intently.

"Today, I'll show you something important," she said her voice old and calm like the crags surrounding the compound. "Go and say goodbye to Mrs. Jackson first." There was a gleam in her eyes that reminded me of something, but I couldn't remember what exactly that thing was, not even if my life depended on it. I'd seen that deep green glitter before.

She walked slowly, her walking stick hitting the sand and leaving yellow whirlwinds in her wake. I suddenly thought I hadn't asked what her name was. Then I thought I wanted to live. Couldn't I run away from that awful place? I imagined the word "dead" written in front of my name in the monthly report Boris would submit to the Center.

I would be a disgrace to my family, a deserter. I would be a curse to my whole native town. Well, I had no family. My mother had died. I'd leave no one behind me, and no one would miss me. Perhaps Mrs. Jackson would leave a small glass of whiskey for me on her table. I hoped she wouldn't let another guy touch it. The cheap brandy made her so beautiful I could cry. Yes, I wanted to see her, talk to her, live for her. She came closest to my idea of caring for someone. I wanted to get drunk with her one more time.

"Shall we go?" the old woman said as she led the way, her stick barely touching the sand.

"Where are you taking him?" Brits yelled.

The old woman hadn't started for the green stream; she had turned her back to the hill. She walked slowly, taking her time, her stick dragging like a dying lizard at her feet. I was surprised when she chose a path I knew too well. It wasn't a well-trodden one, and the sand around it was yellowish-red, coarse and abrasive. There were no traces of bare feet on that narrow path. I knew where it led.

"Where are you taking me?" I asked the old woman.

"You should have guessed by now," she answered.

At the foot of a red crag, which looked as if a madman had set it on fire, there was a dilapidated shack. Its walls were heaps of stones, rusty metal pieces and parts of faded plastic containers on which smiling faces had been sketched in charcoal. I knew who had drawn these faces. I had bought the charcoal myself.

"This is Mrs. Jackson's house," I said.

The old woman opened the door and said, "It's about time, Jake."

The only room was the way I remembered it. The sand floor was covered with faded, threadbare mats, and a mattress, very shabby and thin, lay in the corner. There was a blue shirt on the mattress. It was my shirt. I knew the low table in the other corner; I had made it with the boards I stole from the coffin we had bought for John, my roommate. At the time, we didn't know he'd become a handful of dust. No one needed coffins in the compound so I used the boards. There were several cheap glass figures arranged in a neat row on the table: a cat, a goat, another bigger cat. I had given them to Peta when I visited her mother. The girl had taken to whispering the childhood tales I had told her. They were simple and silly tales.

"Jake," the old woman called out, but I didn't want to listen to her. I knew I'd die soon. I felt it.

At school, we had a teacher I had been in love with. She used to tell the class fairy tales. She was the only human being that had been kind to me, well, she had been kind to all of us and I was kind of jealous of the other kids in the class. I remembered only one of her tales, the one about the sunny princess and her savior. The smiling faces on the walls of the shack were the characters from that funny tale. Peta and Mrs. Jackson had sketched them in charcoal. Mrs. Jackson loved drawing, and she was quite good when she was sober. I often hid the bottle of whiskey she searched for so I could look at her as she sketched smiling faces on the faded plastic containers.

"You're beautiful when you smile, Jake" she'd told me.

I used to like her voice very much. Not that I cared about her. Well, I did. I did care about Mrs. Jackson. I was sorry about the glass she kept on the table for that guy who never showed up. I wished I was him, and sometimes I wished Peta was my child. I knew well an explorer could be no one's father. Explorers vanished without a trace, turned into smoke or into poisonous crystals. Anyway, I'd always hated that nonsense.

Once again, I sensed I was going to die soon.

"Jake," the old woman said.

This time I glanced at her.

The old woman waited at the table looking closely at me. Mrs. Jackson and her daughter little Peta stood behind her. When had they come here, and how? I hadn't heard any noise. I knew there was no backdoor to the only room of the shack.

Then I was suddenly aware of something: their green eyes, the green glitter that I had noticed every time the old woman had talked to me. It was defiant and gentle at the same time. That quiet, dark green light had waited for me when I drank Mrs. Jackson's brandy, that emerald glow in the eyes of the child when I told her the only fairy tale I knew.

"You still don't understand?" It was Mrs. Jackson that spoke to me.

"Don't push him," the little girl said. "Don't make it hard on him. Hey, Jake! Look at us. Look at our faces."

I did what I was told and I found out nothing of interest.

"Don't we look similar to you, Jake?"

Their faces did look similar, the high forehead, the chiseled cheekbones, the lips, the eyebrows, and that quiet glitter in their eyes.

"We *are* the hill, Jake," said the old woman.

The three of them looked at me.

"We are the hill," Mrs. Jackson repeated. "The hill … that means one can be young and old at the same time, Jake."

"Try to understand," the old woman went on as she sat down on the mattress. "One is dying and one is being born at the same time."

"What?" I breathed.

What she'd just said didn't make any sense. No sense at all.

"One is getting old and getting younger at the same time, Uncle Jake," Peta said smiling at me. "I loved your fairy tale about the sun princess. I so much wanted you to become like us. We can change the end of the fairytale together."

"The three of us are one and the same person," the old woman breathed. "I am the old age, Peta is the child, and she ...," the old woman turned to Mrs. Jackson, "you know what she is."

"This is crazy," I breathed though I was trained to never make comments about hills. The hill destroys you unless you destroy it. That was what Boris had taught me. I sensed death approaching.

"Are you ... death?" I whispered.

"We are a hill, Jake," Mrs. Jackson said. "And there are thousands of hills like us."

My feet hurt, my hand hurt, and I could hardly breathe.

"We are freedom, Jake," the old woman said. "It's strange. I like you, and I'm a helpless old thing, and she," the woman pointed to Mrs. Jackson. "She loves you. She ... she is stupid and she loves you. You can take my word for that."

"I love you, too, Uncle Jake," the girl shouted. "I want you to come and play with me. I love the glass cats you gave me."

Wait, I said to myself. Wait! All this is crazy. I'm going mad.

"Peta, you screamed at night and my friend Simon died in the morning," I said. "Why did you do that?" I breathed with difficulty, trying hard to keep my sanity.

It was warm in the room, and it was quiet and I hated it. The old woman, Mrs. Jackson, and little Peta exchanged glances.

"Tell him, honey," Mrs. Jackson said.

"That man wanted to set the hill on fire, all your friends did," Peta said. "They crossed the stream and burned some of the trees. And if a tree burns, then I burn, too."

"I'm as old as the hills and I know," the old woman said. "I help Peta, and I can help Mrs. Jackson and they help me. See?"

"It's much easier to be a child and a woman at the same time. You are never lonely. You have always someone to talk to."

"But you killed John, and you killed Simon," I groaned.

"No, they are hills now," the old woman said. "But they can't cross the stream back to the compound."

"So, they are as good as dead?" I asked looking at her face that was as old as the dry valley and as sad. "I will never see them again." Then a weird thought crossed my mind. Why did they take me here? Did they want me dead? I wished I could see the green stream again. I wanted to see the sunset.

"Why did you take me here?" I asked. "I haven't set fire to your hill. I did nothing wrong."

The green glitter in their eyes appeared strange in the semi darkness.

The old woman turned her head to Mrs. Jackson and said, "She didn't want to return to the hill, the silly woman. She fell in love with you. She wanted to get old with you and never become young again."

"No, no, Uncle Jake," little Peta interrupted her. "I don't want to go back to the hill, too. I want to stay with you. You tell me that beautiful tale. Uncle Jake! You can be a child. I'll teach you how to become a child whenever you want. It's easy. And you can be an old man. She will teach you." the child pointed to the old woman.

I reached out and touched Mrs. Jackson's hand. Her face was so beautiful I could hardly breathe. I looked through the narrow window and I saw the hill in the distance.

"I want to be with you," Mrs. Jackson said. There were tears in her eyes, the most beautiful eyes I had seen.

"That glass that you put on the table," I muttered. "That glass you didn't let me touch. That glass on the table ... who did you keep it for?"

She didn't answer for a long time. Then I knew it would difficult for me to live without her. I couldn't live without the green lonely glitter in her eyes.

"That glass was meant ... for ... for the impossibility of it ..." the old woman suddenly said. "She loves you. Love is impossible. I should know, believe me. I lived through it. Love is impossible to happen."

"It is possible," Mrs. Jackson breathed.

The sand valley was a long sigh in the air, and life was a long sand valley that had seen no rain for months. Life was green glitter that would run dry.

"You lived through it?" I said looking at the old face that was a lonely dune waiting for the wind.

"Yes, I know you, Jake. I know you very well. The impossibility of it …" the old woman said slowly.

***

An old man, quite tall, his wild white hair tousled, trudged limping through the sand dunes. A couple of yards behind him a boy, puny, as thin as a lath, carrying a stick in his dirty hand, tried to run and catch up with the old man. It was very hot, the boy soon got tired, his steps became uncertain, he staggered and fell. The old man didn't look back. Another man, youngish, or perhaps middle-aged, ran to the child and reached out to help him get up.

"Jake," Boris shouted. "Hey, Jake."

The middle-aged man didn't answer. He held the puny child by the hand and said something to the old geezer.

"Hey, Jake, who are these people with you? Jake. Jake!"

The valley was so quiet one could hear a pin drop.

"Where have you been?" Boris shouted. He'd already gone into one of his huffs.

"Jake! Jake!"

Neither Jake nor the old man said a word. The boy smiled and looked at the brown hill.

The Brandy Maker

"No need to hurry, sir," I said. "You can't kill me no matter how hard you try."

My worst enemy, Long Joe, was pressing his knife against my throat, and I saw droplets of blood trickling down my new blouse. My words failed to impress him as the sharp blade sank deeper into my flesh.

"Stop it," I groaned. "I'll show you my gravestone."

It was very hot, the sand burned under my feet, the stones were red-hot and there were several blackbirds that had dropped dead in the heat, little crusts of dried blood under their heads. The heat stank of decay, Joe's sour breath was all over my face and his blade carved deeper into my neck. The drops of blood that trickled from the wound turned into rusty crusts on my new blouse.

"I don't believe in gravestones," Joe snarled.

"Look at my gravestone first," I managed to say, a dangerous thought crossing my mind. What if that old man who corrected my gravestone was a cheat? My neck hurt. I had to brace up.

"Joe," I said, "you know what happens to a guy who doesn't respect a gravestone. They find him cold and dead."

I had already choked on the fetid air, and it seemed impossible to pull myself together. Swallowing hard, I grunted, "The hyenas eat the face first then gnaw on the bones. That's what happens to the man who has no respect for the gravestones."

The knife that had dug into my throat slipped away.

"I see you understand, Joe," I said.

When a child was born in the little villages in the desert, the parents took their baby to the dilapidated gray shack which was not far from my dugout. The old man who lived in it gave the parents a gravestone for their child. It was an ordinary slab of sandstone on which the old geezer chiseled the kid's date of birth and the date of death. The parents put the slab in front of their home. I'd never heard that someone died before his date of death or that he lived longer than the date the old man had carved on the gravestone.

Joe was my bitterest competitor. We both made brandy from the thorns we collected in the desert. He was much stronger than me, and he crawled deeper into the biting hot dunes, muttering curses under his breath. I'd seen his thin shadow flitting like a vulture over the sand, a huge sack of precious thorns on his back. The desert stretched miles on end, brown and yellow, strewn with dead birds and dead lizards. I'd heard Joe put lizards in his brandy to kill its acrid taste. I didn't put anything in mine. My brandy was worse than his, but it was cheap, dirt cheap, and I was wealthier than Joe. I thought I could buy his business and make him one of my laborers.

"I'll kill you," he snarled. "It's a shame you make more money than me. You are a woman, damn you."

The sky was the desperate blue color of evaporating moisture and looking at it made me sick at heart. At least you are still alive, I thought to myself. You're alive and kicking in the heat.

"You steal the thorns your laborers gather," Joe said bringing me back to his sharp knife and the scorched drops of blood on my blouse. "And you are mean."

"I don't steal their horns," I countered. "They give them to me of their own accord."They all were desperate men who drank my brandy. There were no women miles and miles around, and the hole I had dug in the sand was deep and cool at night. I was mean, yes, I was very mean. I took the thorns the guy had been collecting for weeks and I let him spend the night with me in my deep cool hole. In the morning, I gave him all cheap brandy he could drink. My brandy was sharp and good, and the guy had earned every drop of it.

No one had ever asked me how much I had to endure. The heat, the sweat, the scorching sun, and the nights with men I didn't like. The two guys I called Jim One and Jim Two, my laborers, were both cruel and rude. No one asked if it was easy for me to curb their warped imaginations, to give them pleasures, and make them speak to me respectfully, "Yes, Madam, No, Madam." I hated to think how much it cost me to wrench precious thorns from thirsty men and live on trying not to remember they'd come back to kill me. I had to be ready for the next bag of dried withered thistles. The guy who kissed me could slit my throat if he wanted to.

"Well, I am richer than you and I am mean, but I am no coward, Joe," I said.

"And your brandy tastes good," he muttered.

Some guys I knew said they didn't believe in their gravestones, others fretted they had only a couple of years more to live. They bought my thorn brandy and drank for days until I shouted I had nothing more to offer them. I lied, of course. I always had brandy. Most of my customers dropped stone drunk in front of my hole and if I left them there the heat and the sun would kill them.

At the beginning, Jim One and Jim Two had tried to make brandy themselves, but they wanted a woman so badly and so often they ended up in my hole, their sacks of thorns becoming mine in a matter of hours.

Long Joe hated my customers, he called them thugs and he called me bitch, but day in and day out he dragged his huge sacks of thorns to my dugout. The thistles and burrs he brought were bigger and juicier than those of my laborers and he said, "You'll make twice as much brandy from these. I'll stay three nights in your hole instead of one."

He had threatened me with his knife many times. He tattooed his name, JOE, on my back and said, "Don't you dare forget it!" Other guys had tattooed their names on my back, too, and he hated that. He knew I made very good brandy from his huge thorns and wanted to know where I hid it. I never told him. He was a strong man. After him, I needed a good rest before I took to looking for thorns myself.

"Show me your gravestone," Joe said.

I showed it to him. It was an ordinary battered slab of sandstone with my name chiseled on it. Joe looked at it and heaved a deep sigh.

"You have thirty-five years more to live," he said.

"You see I told you the truth," I said. "You can't kill me now. Don't even try."

"Give me brandy," he thundered.

There were times when I was afraid of his enormous voice. It rendered me motionless with horror and made my blood freeze. Then, gradually, I got accustomed to it. I let him roar and howl and wail. He couldn't kill me, I knew. My gravestone was a proof I'd live longer than his huge voice.

"I can beat you black and blue," he said. "I can break your legs and you'll crawl like a crippled lizard. You'll smell like a crushed cockroach."

"Yes, you can do that," I said. "But there's no other woman in these parts. Would you like to spend the night with a crippled woman, one that can't kiss the way she should and one that can't love you the way she should?"

"I shouldn't have let you come here," he grumbled.

"It's a free desert," I said. "We all have our gravestones to take care of."

"I don't believe in gravestones, damn you," Joe shouted. "You make me drink your foul swill, but this time I won't have it. I haven't come here to get drunk. I've come for you."

"As you wish," I said. "I understand. Let me see your thorns first and please give me your knife. The wound you carved in my neck will take a week to heal."

He grunted and then showed me the thorns. This time he'd brought three sacks of marvelous juicy thistles with small purple berries at the end of each thick barb-like leaf. I couldn't believe my eyes; these were precious, superb thorns. I could make golden brandy from them. Then perhaps I could visit once again to the cabin of that geezer, the gravestone maker.

"Come on, pay me," Joe snarled.

"You have to respect a woman who will live as long as me," I said. "If you don't hurt me I'll teach you to love a woman the way you should."

"Shut up," he thundered.

Well, I would make him wait. I'd make him wait until he screamed. Thorns or no thorns, love was precious and I had to teach him to respect it.

"I have to pray first," I said.

"Pray? What for?" he asked.

"That's none of your business."

I had to learn not to be afraid of Joe. He brought me the best thorns, it was true, but he was savage and his somber moods made me feel creepy. He carved his name on my back because he was furious. He hated it when I called him Jim the way I called all men who happened to bring me thorns and spend the night with me.

"Come on," Joe roared. "I hate waiting."

"I'm still praying," I said.

"Stop it!"

"I'm still praying," I said.

I didn't pray. Every time Joe brought his marvelous thorns, declaring he'd stay three nights in my hole, I remembered the old man I'd visited, the gravestone maker. The memory of his shack killed the panic Joe had sent racing down my spine.

My gravestone was a cheap piece of sandstone which I could carry with utmost difficulty. I didn't mind it was so heavy. The date of birth and the date of death chiseled on it told me I'd live thirty-four years. It was true the desert was an abominable nightmare of heat, poisonous snakes, and dead hot sands. It was true my hole was a narrow one, and I had to walk miles before I found precious thorns. It was true down-and-out men gave me thorns for my love. It was true I was mean, and I didn't deserve to live more than my gravestone told me I would.

But I loved the desert, I loved the endless motionless heaps of angry sand, and I loved the quiet of the nights. I even loved the down-and-out losers who gave me their thorns and their inability to become rich. I taught them to respect love. I was not ashamed of the scars they'd left on my skin, and I was proud I was the only woman amidst the wild dunes. I wanted to live longer.

I went to the gravestone maker's shack. It took me three days and three nights of trudging through the sands, three days and three nights of dragging my battered gravestone, beaten out of shape by the sandstorms. Years ago, I had thrown it out of my hole, I was so angry my mother had not tried to negotiate somewhat longer life for me.

I entered the shack and I saw the old man at work, a heavy hammer in hand. He wore a mask and I wondered why he wanted to hide his face. Was it that ugly? Did he wear the mask to protect himself from the dust in the shack? The man didn't look up. I waited and waited, and he worked on, tapping and hitting the stone. The shack was a tumble-down affair, made of sticks and bone-dry poles. I hated it.

"Good afternoon, sir," I said as I laid my gravestone at my feet. He didn't say anything.

I had taken thorns from surly men, raw like deathly winds in a sandstorm, and I was not frightened by them. I turned their rudeness into obedience, and I transformed their greed into soft kisses.

"Sir,'" I said, "I brought you this."

He looked up his eyes behind the mask like rattlesnakes.

"I brought you my gravestone, Sir," I said. "Can you correct the date of death, please?"

"What?" the man roared.

His thunderous voice made the shack shake, but I was a woman who collected thorns in the big burning valleys of death, a girl who made brandy and tamed wild men, one who converted fetid heat to wealth and prosperity. And my brandy was something that beat the poison of the rattlesnakes. My skin made men obedient.

"I'll give you something that will make you happy, sir," I said, producing a tiny bottle of thorn brandy from my breast pocket.

"Do you know who I am?" the man with the mask asked.

"I bring you something that will make you happy whoever you are," I said as I opened the bottle. "It's not poisonous. I'll drink some of it so you can see."

The man took the bottle from me and took a swig. First, he coughed, for the brandy had the desert and the stormy winds in it, then he brushed his mouth under the mask and took another swig.

"Do you have more of this?" he asked.

"Yes, sir," I said as I produced another bottle. "Give me your word you'll correct my gravestone."

"I won't correct your gravestone," he said.

I shook the bottle under his nose.

The man didn't wait for me to hand it to him. He grabbed it, extricated the stopper with his teeth, then drank thirstily, my brandy spilling over his mask and wetting it.

"Do you have more?" he asked, his rumbling voice sounding kind of merry and the desert felt as if it was about to start raining.

"Here you are," I said giving him more of my brandy. I had treated many men to it, surly man who shouted and drank and then they were as happy as lizards basking in the sun.

"You wanted me to correct the date of your death?" the man said.

"Yes, sir."

"Let me see your gravestone."

After the man gave me my gravestone back, I could hardly believe my eyes. He'd given me fifty more years to live, fifty more endless summers in the scorching sun of the desert, fifty thousand nights of full moon with my thorn brandy and the surly men I had to teach to respect love.

"Thank you, sir," I stammered, still unbelieving.

Then a quick thought crossed my mind.

"Sir, you were so kind. Would you like me to bring you more of ... of this?" I showed him another bottle. "Perhaps you could correct the gravestones of my friends?" I was thinking of the churlish men who drank my brandy, the guys who spent the nights in my narrow hole. These were poor devils I happened to love.

"I know where you live," the man with the mask said. "If I want more brandy, I'll come and have some."

"What?" I asked. "You don't know where I live."

"I know everything," The man with the mask rumbled. "Go way before I correct your gravestone once again."

"You prayed too long!" That was Long Joe shouting at me. "I'm sick of waiting for you."

"Joe," I said. "You have to wait. You have to respect a woman even if she is a mean bitch like me."

"I brought you the best thorns in the desert," he said. "Come here or give me back my knife. I'll need it to cut your throat."

"Your knife," I repeated, feeling suddenly hot pain where he had cut me. "Joe, you can't kill me. Didn't I make that clear? My gravestone says I have many more years to live. Do you care to see it?"

"You don't want to show me your date of death," Long Joe said.

"Why, because you don't believe in gravestones?" I jeered.

It was hot in my dugout. I knew that sand dunes were red-hot and the sky was so blue I could not look at it.

"Look at me," Joe ordered. "Come on, look at me." He produced a mask and hid his angular face behind it. ``Don't you recognize me now?"

I looked at him.

"Are you ... you are ..." I stammered remembering the gray decrepit shack, the sandstones and the man who hammered and tapped on them. "You ... you make the gravestones? And you decide how long we live?" I ventured.

"Come here quick," Joe said. His voice didn't rumble or thunder. It was a happy voice, a voice that had learned to respect a woman who made thorn brandy in the red desert.

"You are wilder than your brandy," the man said slowly.

Nadya

Bliss was approaching. You recognized it in your bones, the tourists said. They added that you knew it was there because you couldn't sleep at night. There was that pleasant itching in your skin. The Hole was an old little place that had nothing interesting about it. Soon, people became accustomed to the odd mountains that rose and fell apart under their feet during Bliss. Bliss ended and the shuddering hills vanished. The mountain chains turned into flat and dull plains which slept serenely until the next Bliss. Then the land swelled without warning, hills jumped out of the blue, mounds jutted out, wriggled and writhed before they all evaporated without a trace. The squirming hills made no difference to the tourists.

The precious thing about the Hole was Bliss. You observed no laws—you simply did whatever you pleased, the tourists bragged. You could slit anybody's throat. Blood made no difference, they knew, for during Bliss no one could die. Tourists admitted that they felt pain, yes, but neither they nor the targets they chose met their maker. Death was virtually non-existent because guys like me collected the mutilated bodies and took them to the healing plateau.

The plateau regenerated ripped intestines, slashed chests, and torn viscera. Bliss made you kill and kiss, the wealthy tourists told me. Nothing compared to that bliss. You just had to catch the fragrance of Bliss. That was easy to do. Bliss didn't make me feel its fragrance. It only made me hate Jar Girls Hotel.

I didn't want to be a body collector anymore, but there was big money in it.

There was a jar on my cupboard I looked at day and night. That jar made me feel crazy. There is hope, I said to myself. There is still hope she might be back. There's still hope. That was why I didn't leave the Hole.

Nadya.

It was the tag sewn to the collar of her shirt that made it clear she was one of the regulars. "Nadya," her tag said. It had three blue notches on it and that meant she'd been at the holidaymakers' beck and call three consecutive Bliss spells. That was an awful lot.

She was pretty, of course. All the regulars were. Women, children, men, all were very attractive. I'd been working as a body collector in the Hole for years and not a single body of a regular target was plain. The healing plateau rejected dirty bodies, squashed chests or disfigured faces, but it readily took on bodies without fingers, hands, or eyes. I was greedy. They paid well for perfectly clean bodies that were in good shape. They took them from you, checked them, then put the bodies on the flat ground. "They" were the cops who protected the holidaymakers' interests. They came here five Bliss spells ago.

Outside Bliss, the Hole was a peaceful place. No hills sprouted from it, and its soil didn't quake. There were no rocks, not even sands. The plateau was smooth like ice. I guessed it was the Hole that exuded the smell that killed the pain and healed the injuries. No one knew for sure. The Hole cured you during Bliss.

"Don't touch me!" Nadya had said.

If the organs of a body were defective you didn't get a cent for your efforts. The healing plateau didn't regenerate sick lungs or infected spleens so I checked the organs myself and replaced the malfunctioning ones. It was worth it. I had a lot of money; unfortunately, a lot was never enough. I wanted to buy a plot from the Hole, and I could well afford it. I was the richest body collector in this part of the world. Nadya was screaming in pain when I found her. There was nothing extraordinary about that. She was one of the regulars, and they all screamed. They came to the Hole, lured by the prospect of quick money.

I felt kind of sorry for them. Some rich clients had favorite regulars and booked them well in advance. Often clients and regulars got drunk together, waiting for Bliss. The regulars had contracts and everything was perfectly legal, even experimental sex. The Hole cured all regular targets, and no one died.

When I saw Nadya, I froze in my tracks. I knew.

Nadya's left ear was missing. There was no bleeding, no wound, just healthy pink rims where normally an ear should be. There simply was no ear. At a certain point, I caught the thin, sweet smell of the ocean. Few could catch the smell of the ocean in the Hole.

I could. And I knew what the smell meant.

The Insurance Agency paid me to find the bodies of the wealthy clients and take good care of them while I dragged them to the healing plateau. The clients paid me, too. They wanted me to have their organs inspected because an injured organ caused wrinkles on the cheeks, hardly visible wrinkles, it was true, but rich guys hated them all the same. I made big money doing something dangerous for the big shots and they paid me most dearly to ward them off from the water.

The healing air was helpless before the ocean of the Hole.

The water was transparent. It dissolved everything that fell into it: shoes, hair, bones, and bodies—no matter how rich their owners were. The bigwigs paid me to steer them clear from the ocean. I often grabbed them before they collapsed from a mountain that squirmed under their feet; sometimes the land split and water gushed out from the hideous crack. The bad thing was that the Hole could not regenerate any tissue that the ocean had dissolved. I tried once. I dissolved a wisp of Nadya's hair in a jug of water.

Sometimes strange things happened. When Bliss began and hills popped up, quaking and breaking as if the land were a river, I heard somebody say, "Take me out of the plateau."

I recognized the voice. It was Nadya's. I thought I was only dreaming or hallucinating. The voice kept on mouthing the same words—now crooning, now raving. I recorded it, trying to rule out the crawling suspicion that it was my imagination shouting at Bliss.

Body collectors often went crazy. Ordinary guys feared us and said we, the collectors, were freaks. We were greedy and mercenary. I was the greediest among them.

Yes, Nadya's voice was there, real and soft, recorded by the most expensive equipment you could buy in the Hole. One day I threw out the jug in which I had dissolved a wisp of her hair. My hut was cozy but inexpensive. I could never be sure when a hill would push its way up to the sky under the floor of my living room, destroying my home in a matter of seconds. The day after I threw out the jug, the steep slopes around my hut screamed at me, "Take me out of the plateau!" The hill where I poured the water became Nadya's voice.

After a week of screaming, the hill broke, ripping open the valley, and I saw a figure in the blue distance. It was Nadya. She approached me, looking beautiful, so beautiful I forgot everything else, the wiggling hills, the stalking valleys, the rich clients and their targets. Then all was quiet. Nadia was gone, the hills disappeared. Bliss had come to its end. Ends came abruptly, without warning. They always took me by surprise. There were no mountains, no quaking ridges, and gorges; the ocean was peaceful dead water I could swim in with some of the regulars. I got drunk with them. I often made love to the prettiest women free of charge. That was illegal, of course.

Nadya was different. She'd been collected three times before I stumbled upon her. I could smell a dying man from two miles. I could feel the moment when the mountain would crash down, interring the bodies—my only hope of getting rich. I sensed the tremor before the crests of the hills ripped the low sky. I fought the dust that suffocated the regulars and marred their bodies.

Nadya was pretty, but if you were pretty and a woman you were in store for a hard time. Wealthy clients booked you as a target. Their lawyers paid you a lot to keep quiet. Pretty women were desperate for money. I worked for a client who paid me to scoop a pail of water from the ocean then he made his target dip her foot in the pail. The water dissolved the foot in a flash and remained clear, transparent, quiet. A scream rent the air; that was the target's scream, but only experienced body collectors could distinguish it amidst the roar of the rising and folding mountains. I had found eleven women's bodies without feet. I did my best to make the missing foot grow again. I kept the bodies for a week on the healing plateau. Nothing came out of that. I had made love to women who had lost their hands.

"You can't imagine the ecstasy during intimate contacts after that," one woman, a client, told me.

"After what?" I asked her.

"I think the target's ear I dissolved gave the water great excitement. My sex life improved incredibly after I drank that water." I was an avaricious man, a very avaricious one. My client was very rich.

"What was your target's name?" I asked her out of curiosity.

"As a rule, I don't ask my targets their names," she answered. "But this time the girl was particularly good looking. Her name was Nadya." I froze in my tracks.

"Do you think I can convince Nadya to dip her breasts into the water for me?" she asked.

I hit the woman. I hit her hard.

It was the first time I hit a client in my life.

I knew Nadya had only one toe on her right foot.

"Doesn't it feel awkward that way? Doesn't it hurt?" I had asked her when I took her out to the healing plateau.

"No," she said. "I feel no pain at all."

"You gave that bitch four of your toes," I said. "You should have made a fortune by now."

"A fortune is not enough," she said. "I want to buy the Hole. I want all of it, its Bliss spells and its nasty water." A smile crept on her lips. "Then I'll blow it up."

"You're crazy," I told her.

"I am," she whispered.

Then we made love. It had never been so beautiful with other women, maybe because I was sorry for her. Loving her was like loving the wind. She didn't feel like a regular. She was gentle and brittle. She was lovely. I had rarely felt sorry for anybody before.

"I have a bad headache," Nadya had said. "My head throbs. Please, kiss me on the forehead."

I kissed her forehead. It was smooth like a child's. Then she fell asleep.

"My headache is gone," she said when she woke up. "It's good when you kiss me."

"I don't want you to go with other clients," I heard myself saying. I didn't mean to. The words escaped my lips. Thank God she didn't say anything. Imagine a toeless regular sobbing on your shoulder. I hated the thought of it. Thank God she had kept silent then.

"Why do you want me to take you out of the healing plateau?" I asked. In the beginning, I was just curious. I guessed she made a lot of money. The clients paid generously if you agreed to let your toes dissolve into the water.

"Have you ever been on the healing plateau?" she whispered.

"No," I said.

"I've been there a dozen times." She sat up, staring at the wasteland of blue sands that was as flat as the ocean.

"How does it feel on the plateau?" I asked. She said nothing for a long time.

"Kiss me on the forehead," she suddenly pleaded, trembling. "Please, kiss me. That headache ..."

It was the first time in my life it had felt sweet to touch human skin. I knew skin cost a lot. I often replaced parts of my client's faces, and I chose good new skin for them. Nadya's skin was odd. I could swear there were ripped hills and flat valleys in it. There was fear and sorrow in that skin.

I could have asked her to stay with me. Back then I thought she'd make no difference. She was another vanishing hill, another body I'd take money for. I didn't know she was the only woman whose headache I could turn into peace. I didn't know I'd miss the blue valleys in her skin. I didn't know I'd miss the disappearing hill only because she had walked on it, making it her hill.

The body collectors were a tough lot. I was pretty tough, too. Nadya asked me, "Can I stay with you? I'll clean your hut, and I'll build it again when the Hole breaks it. I'll cook for you."

"How can you cook?" I asked her. "You can't walk quickly. You don't have enough toes on your feet. You stagger."

I hated it when someone touched my things, my expensive equipment. I was afraid she might steal something. Women were cheap. Each cost less than the tent that protected my bodies from getting dirty in the dust of the rumbling hills.

"Okay," she said. "I'll go. I hope you'll be happy with your equipment."

"We may meet during the next Bliss," I told her. "You know where you can find me. I always build my hut near the healing hotel." It was so quiet, a deep transparent peace that was the most precious thing in the Hole. When Bliss was over, there were no tourists and no clients, no sick people who flew to the Hole hoping that Bliss would last forever. There was no death in the Hole during Bliss.

"Kiss me on the forehead," she said. "You'll do me a favor, and it won't cost you anything."

Her skin was smooth—it tasted of the ocean and the deep quiet. The mountains had vanished, and the planet was an endless blue plain. Nadya didn't even say good-bye. I watched her go, thinking of the red, healthy-looking rims on the spot where her ear should be. Suddenly she turned around and whispered, "I think I love you."

That was a silly thing to say. Love was as cheap as the specks of dust on the infinite plain.

Another Bliss spell came and ended. I made even more money, and I could now buy a plot in the Hole. I hoped I'd meet Nadya. I wondered how she coped with her headaches. I felt like climbing the hills she had slept on. I asked my clients if they'd met a thin woman with disfigured feet, yes, three or four toes missing. She'd lost an ear, too.

"You don't tell me anything in particular," the clients answered me. "All regular female targets look like the one you've just described."

"Her name is Nadya," I said, realizing how stupid I'd been. You came to the Hole to dissolve your target's fingers in the water. Her name hardly mattered at all. I had enough money, and I could hire a private eye, but that would be ludicrous. No one searched for women in the Hole.

One day a big boat stopped in front of my hut. Bliss was just over, and there were no tourists, no clients. It was the spell of deep quiet when all mountains were dead.

A woman entered. She hadn't knocked on the door. I knew that woman. That was the only client I had hit in my long career of a body collector.

"This is Nadya," she said and lifted a jar half full of transparent liquid under my nose. "My husband drank the rest of her. Our sex life is glorious now."

I looked at the jar the woman was holding in her hands. It was big and round, perfectly transparent. I looked at the woman. She was small and plump, her face round and smirking. Then I suddenly knew what her face reminded me of.

It was like the flat, dead outlines of the Hole.

I didn't know how it happened. Maybe the hills were to blame, I wasn't sure. Maybe a mountain spilled some water out of the jar as it pushed its way to the clouds. Maybe in an unthinking moment, I poured it out of the window, or maybe another girlfriend of mine, another regular target, spilled the water in a fit of jealousy.

When the hills started to quake and wriggle, dust rose from the beach. The dust over the hill spoke. "Kiss me on the forehead. The headache."

The dust was Nadya's voice

"Kiss me on the forehead!"

The Make-Up Artist

The minute I set foot in the Hole, the border control agents stamped the letter C on the palm of my left hand.

"Why are you doing that?" I asked.

Sara, the girl who sat next to me on the shuttle, got the letter A on her hand, and after we passed the border control a bunch of guys rushed toward her. They grinned radiantly at her after she said she needed help. They all were only too happy to oblige. Sara's perfection rendered them speechless. Their fatuous smiles didn't surprise me at all. Back in our hometown, the first reaction of the male population was exactly the same no matter where Sara and I went. Men adored her. Then a moment came when she opened her mouth and said something. The admiring audience, though stunned by her startling beauty, stared. Sara's intelligence was very modest indeed.

For that reason, Sara ran to me the minute her next boyfriend broke with her. I made her promise she wouldn't jump to another whirlwind romance. However, she could do without romance only when she slept at the back of my studio. The minute she woke up she remembered the guy she had kissed a couple of days ago and cried her eyes out. A hearty meal was all she needed for it made her strong enough to love again.

I was a make-up artist, not a brilliant one, I'd give anyone that, and my clientele dwindled at a disheartening speed. My unfaithful clients were the basic reason that forced me to seek refuge in the Hole, that little place of ill repute. I studied the business catalog of the Hole and I packed up all my belongings. To my utter astonishment, I discovered there were no make-up studios in the darned thing, a fact which would have spoken volumes to a cleverer woman than me. I should have felt there was something fishy going on there. My dreams to get rich quick were the root of all evil in my life.

I took with me all my mascara bottles, my boxes of rouge and powder, all packed up in my enormous suitcase.

I took loans from all my relatives and friends optimistic enough to lend me money. My financial resources were quite negligible, though—a fact explaining why Sara and I were off to the Hole two weeks after I read the advertisement about it in the local paper. Whatever the reason, Sara got a letter A on her wrist while the agent, a strapping guy who hardly spared me a glance, stamped a C on the back of my hand.

"What is this handsome guy doing?" Sara wanted to know. "Why the hell did he scribble those signs on our hands? Hey, Mister," she shouted. "Who do you think you are?"

The agent didn't answer her question. He simply led Sara to a very big and bright staircase moving skyward to a beautifully lit building which shone like a movie theater. More and more border-control agents came, all spruce and elegant in their dazzling uniforms, all smiling at Sara as if she was made of gold, every inch of her scraggy torso. I liked the iridescent rolling staircase on which she proudly stepped, and I was thrilled that so many young men in chic uniforms were nearby. Forgetting all discretion, I rushed toward my bird-brained friend.

"Hey, Miss," one particularly neat agent shouted as he seized my hand, "where do you think you're going?"

"Get your hands off me!" I said. "I'll go wherever I want and you will not stop me."

"I can say you are a C, Madam, so step off the staircase, please."

"I am a C, so what?" I remonstrated, furious. "Let me go."

"Ha, ha," he said and let go of my wrist.

I rushed once again toward Sara. All I managed to do was to take a couple of steps, then, without any apparent reason, the ground opened under my feet and I flopped onto a conveyer belt which started rolling. The darned thing was taking me away from the dazzling light of the skyscraper, from the attractive men, and from my poor friend Sara.

"Hey, hey," I shouted, but no one seemed to take interest in me.

Soon the conveyer belt chucked me in the middle of well-lit empty space, then the rubber surface under my feet vanished as if it had never been there. A man dressed in a dreadful old-fashioned suit showed up from a decrepit building. He came up to me and, uttering no sound at all, grabbed my dress and attempted to tear off its collar.

"What are you doing?" I asked but he went on pulling at my clothes, offering no explanation at all. I caught him unawares and gave him a punch in the nose and tried to run away, but he took out a torch and flashed it in my eyes. Within a second, all my clothes turned into dust and slid down my body. I felt itchy all over. The man didn't seem to be impressed by that.

I had always thought my body was irresistible. Men had praised it and had gone into raptures at its perfection. The guy in the old-fashioned suit pointed the torch at me, driving its light from my toes up my knees, thighs, belly, breasts, and shoulders until he reached my ears. I was astounded. After a minute, he gave me a small plastic card, on which the word HEALTHY was engraved. The card had all biochemical data about me: blood type, the levels of sugar and cholesterol in my blood, the levels of different hormones, including information about my libido which, at that moment, was very low indeed.

Then the man spoke for the first time, "You are a C. Please, keep the card I gave you. Show it to our law enforcement agents in case they demand it from you. You are entitled to 1.3 liters of water per day, and 45 minutes of solar light every fifty hours."

The man didn't bother to look at me as he spoke as if I was a lump of dry mud.

"Your daily allowance of food amounts to 99 KK," he said.

I was standing before him, a woman with an almost perfect body, and the blockhead wasn't paying attention!

"Please be advised that we would not welcome C offspring in the Hole."

"What are you talking about?" I said. He didn't understand my question or pretended he didn't.

"The amount of solar light corresponds to the low intellectual potential of the C female. We will not invest in developing your potential further."

I choked on my own voice.

"The card I provided for you will give you the code numbers of other C individuals that you might want to meet."

I didn't wait for him to say another word. I clouted him across the side of the head. He gave out a short wail and staggered.

"You are under arrest for offending an A-grade agent," he said as he scrambled to his feet.

"I wonder who gave you that A," I sneered and that was all I could remember.

A squad of impressive, able-bodied lads surrounded me, and I began to realize those guys were very serious about their ludicrous grades. The A graders wore gorgeous tunics of metallic color while some other agents looked shabby in their capes of cheap faded nylon. Why that division, I asked myself.

It was not necessary to rack my brains for a long time.

The A graders looked attractive. Their faces sported regular features, and their complexions were immaculate. They all were so perfect I felt like clawing their pink cheeks and gouging their glittering brown eyes. The miserable agents of lower grades were thin and weedy individuals, all of them eyesores. Some had drooping cheeks; others had enormous noses or ears of bizarre shapes.

Then a thought struck me. The border control agents had given me a C right away. Hadn't they noticed my magnificent body? Why didn't they let me dazzle them with my sparkling wit? Why didn't they give me a chance to prove how clever I was? It turned out I was thinking aloud.

"Because you are not clever, Miss," one of the strapping guys, an A-grader, answered the question I still had not asked out loud. "The individuals who do not possess natural physical beauty are not endowed with brains or rich spirituality. Our system takes care of that. The sun in the Hole gives its rays to the naturally beautiful men and women. It does not invest its precious energy in plain individuals that cannot thrive in a C-environment."

"A sun, which is forty billion light years away from me, decides if I'm beautiful or not?" I seethed. "This is downright dishonest!"

My body was beautiful even under the green light of the street lamp. I noticed that some of the guys from the squad had registered that fact.

"You are under arrest," the guy said flatly preserving his equanimity. The members of the squad surrounded me.

"How come I am under arrest?" I shouted. "I've done nothing wrong."

"You endanger security and peace in the Hole," he said.

I saw right away I had to change my tactics as rapidly as I could if I wanted to make it back to the airport and get out of that little nasty Hole.

"I'm entitled to know the reasons why you gave me a C," I said. "If you are really that keen on the supremacy of law you should explain why I was allocated that humiliating grade."

The guy looked quite embarrassed. He blushed furiously and stared at his toes.

"As an A-grade officer I am expected to behave with proper decorum," he finally said. "I would not discuss the intimate flaws and shortcomings of a female individual even though she is a C grader."

"Oh, please do," I urged him attempting to appease him.

"I am too sensitive and civilized," he said, edging a step away from me. "Having to dwell on intimate drawbacks of a female is a torture to me. However, we attach great importance to honesty in the Hole."

Isn't he a bore, I thought but cleverly enough I kept that to myself. I'll teach you a lesson, you law-abiding A-grade imbeciles.

"You've got freckles all over your face," the squad leader said harshly. Perhaps the expression on my face had drastically changed.

"Freckles are considered chic in my native town," I objected, forgetting for a while my decision to play it soft.

"Your complexion is no good," the commanding officer went on, and I was on the verge of exploding. He thundered on, painstakingly enumerating all my flaws and drawbacks. "Your nose is disproportionately long, your features are irregular, you are too meager, your face is too broad, and your eyes lack luster."

The square slowly filled with inquisitive onlookers, their faces freckled, their noses quite long, their faces either too broad or too narrow, their legs too thin or too thick. They all were, I guessed, C-graders, and they all had one thing in common: they looked pasty, ashen, and sick. It was evident they didn't get enough light or food.

"But this is ludicrous," I said. "One should not be deprived of vitamins because one's nose is long."

"Oh, you are wrong," the squad leader objected. "We are very serious about selection in the Hole. The population here gradually becomes more and more beautiful."

"Beautiful?" I said. "Honestly, I'd say you look neither too beautiful nor overwhelmingly intelligent to me. Your parents should have invested in teaching you good manners."

"My parents invested in my good looks," the guy said proudly. "They hired one of the best genetic engineers to design a beautiful baby for them."

"If you are that baby, their money had not achieved anything worth my admiration," I said. Suddenly, the pasty man and women in the square began clapping their hands. The C-graders in the square stared at him, their eyes a thick impenetrable wall, their tarnished pasty skins an angry sight in the blazing light of the streetlamps.

"She is up to no good," the squad leader turned to his men. "The crowd will become dangerous if we do not do something about her."

I had an idea.

"Please, give me an hour, a mirror, and let me use the things I carry in my bag, sir," I said. "Then you'll see how much your theory is worth."

"No," the A-grade agent declared.

"You said the Hole is the cradle of justice and civilization," I reminded him. "You all will be watching me. Just give me half an hour and a mirror."

"Half an hour. A mirror," the crowd shouted.

The A-grade agents of the squad gathered their heads together. All the eight of them were handsome, I couldn't deny that. What made me mad was that floods of bright illumination fell only onto their faces while the crowd, the freckled noses and biggish mouths, remained in the sickly puddles of light of the lamps.

"Give her a mirror," the C-grade guys shouted and I liked immensely their broad peaky faces.

"Okay," the agent said at last. He nodded coldly and I half expected he'd start enumerating my flaws all over again. "We will watch you closely."

He produced an object which resembled a penknife and dialed some figures on it. The penknife unfolded itself into a thin sheet of perfectly polished metal which reflected my undoubtedly C-grade face.

So far, for more than six years back in my native town, I had eked out a living working my fingers to the bone. All day long I made up faces of fussy women whose husbands didn't earn much money. A dozen nervous teenaged girls were my clients, as well. I was great at my job. There were no better make-up artists in our neighborhood. I toiled in a moderately cheap beauty shop and I barely made enough to keep body and soul together. All my boyfriends so far had not been wealthy. It was my unbound mania to possess expensive things that brought me to this bleached square full of C-grade individuals who stared at me.

I took out my bottles of rouge, my boxes of mascara, my multi-colored powders, and blushers. In a thick circle around me, I arranged all my make-up bottles, the trays with eye-shadows, the armada of my eyebrow pencils, the rainbow palette of my lipsticks and lip glosses and the resplendent array of various sorts of face paint I still had in astounding quantities. The eight A-grade agents all gaped at me. Their commander tried to insinuate I was making use of detrimental and toxic substances, but his toxicity meter glowed green all the time. He poked his nose into the jars and vessels of cosmetic stuff itching to intercept toxic vapors.

I didn't mind that. I worked diligently, paying no attention to his zeal. I used all bottles, jars, and small containers I had in my bag. I put layers upon layers of the finest rouge I had. I used generously my different kinds of lipstick, the gloss, and the eyeshadows. I could hear the crowd around me breathing. I had the feeling I had plastered a ton of make-up on my face and neck. I thought I weighed more than the mountains that loomed large in the distance.

The streetlamps around me all went dead. For a split second, there was no light at all, and the square was entirely dark. I could hear the gasping *A-A-A!* of the crowd. Then there was a powerful gush of dazzling light. The sun shone over me, flooding my absurdly made up face with millions and millions of rays. The sharp yellow light made me dizzy. The C-grade crowd didn't get any of the rays. The agents of the squad who had detained me didn't get much of the sun's light, either. Everything was for me. The pavement under my feet turned most unexpectedly into a conveyer belt which started moving up and up, towards the big radiant hotel where my blond friend Sara was taken after we left the shuttle at the airport.

"Oh, no, I said. No! I want something else."

I jumped off the conveyer belt and I shouted to a woman from the crowd, the first one I happened to catch a glimpse of, "Do you want me to make up your face?"

She was a pale, scraggly girl, but after I spread make-up on her face the strange sun sent the thin woman a flood of its rays.

The crowd around me shouted, roared and howled. Men and women rushed towards me, totally ignoring the eight agents. Strong hands lifted me in the air, the multitude cheered, and a dozen of guys carried me on their shoulders toward the big radiant hotel in the dazzling light of their sun.

The only thing I noticed was the amazed face of the squad leader who looked at me, fascinated, lisping and moaning, "It's a miracle!"

Then he shouted, "Can I ask you out on a date one of these days, Madame?"

The Men She Didn't Know

Bertha had tried this joke so many times that she had got tired of it. She'd enter one of these large clean cafes on Louisa Boulevard, under the big chestnut trees that looked like old gossipy wives, and she'd see a guy sitting at one of the neat tables. She'd choose the table in the brightest corner, then she'd hurry to the stranger who drank his beer, suspecting nothing. She'd take the seat opposite him and she'd blurt out, "Hi Jake, it's you again!"

The guy usually blinked, but Bertha didn't give him a minute to think.

"It was wonderful in Oostende," she'd say. "The sand dunes, the sun, and the marvelous day. You remember what you said to me, Jake?"

"You must be wrong, Miss," the man would say. "I don't know what you speak about," or "I've never been in Oosende, there must be some other guy you met there."

She'd end up in a hotel room with the man that said later, "You are simply wonderful, I am lucky I look like that guy you met in Oostende."

Several days after the hotel room, the man would ask her to dinner, and it would rain. It always rained in Brussels, thick rain that put clouds and streetlamps in her thoughts. Her translations were no good when it rained, and her poems were so odd that after reading a few lines she threw them into a dustbin. She telephoned the poets whose poems she translated into Dutch and she said, "I don't want to read anything anymore." She kept the endless shivering rhythm of the rain in her bones, and the poems she wrote were deserted streets.

It was entirely different if the day was sunny.

"Il va pluvoire, it will rain," the radio said again. Then the poem would be no good, she knew, and there'd be no use translating the gray wet day into a handful of sad verse.

She went out and there would always be a stranger drinking beer at the brightest spot in that old cafe. She chose a man who looked sad, one who smoked and told him "Hi Jake, you remember what we did in Oostende?"

The day they were together in Oostende was warm, she told the guy she'd just met, although the sun wasn't bigger than a Northern seagull. The wind was inquisitive and friendly. In fact, that was the poem she was going to write if it had not started to rain and, "If you had not spoken to me that day," she added looking in the guy's eye. Then Bertha ended up in a hotel room, the man saying, "I love the rain and I like you, please let's go to Oostende because I've never been there."

Bertha didn't want a guy that had never been to Oostende, and her Oostende wasn't at all the town on the North Sea, it was a town in her head where the sun never set and the streets were long, quiet songs. It was a place where she rode her bicycle days on end until the sun set in the pocket of her leather jacket. She wanted a poem as big as the night and a guy as good as that poem. She wanted to stay with him, but not in a hotel room, she wanted to stay with him in his life that would be as good as a shadow of a smile. That would be impossible, she knew, for every man was a betrayal of some sort.

After, "You are pretty," the guy said he had to go home. It was much better that way. Bertha didn't want a man for herself that couldn't give her Oostende with the sun on the harbor, and a heart as big as a sunset.

All she wanted from the men she didn't know was a crazy story about the North Sea. All she did for the men she ended up with in a hotel room with was to write a poem for them.

These were very short poems scribbled on odd pieces of paper she tore from old calendars, from notebooks, or posters. She collected those scraps of paper in an old basket, and she didn't remember the faces of the men, she remembered the stories they told her about the happiest days of their lives. She began the poems she wrote with the words the man had said to her, "You are a drop of tired water", "You are a bitch, you are pretty and lost, you are the most magnificent lie in my life." It rained in all the poems she wrote.

Bertha wanted an impossible man in her Oostende where it took a lifetime to say hello.

The scraps of paper in that old basket became more numerous and that was how her poetry came to be. It was different when she wrote poems in Dutch. She had another basket in which she put the poems which began with the words she had said to the men who had never been in Oostende.

"See you tomorrow at the same time, on the same quay," she'd say to these men.

Bertha never went to the same quay and that was a way it always ended. "On the same quay" meant "never." After the same quay, she was free like the rain that drove away the tourists and left the beach clean for a new poem.

Some of the men she'd written poems for tried to find her, and she had to tell them, "Tomorrow on the same quay," but she never wrote the same poem twice and never invited a man to her Oostende again. A poem was all she could do for a man. Then she left him in her old basket because she was kind and compassionate, and she was grateful the man was a poem in her life. There were many beautiful poems there, in her rainy days, and she loved them all.

One day she entered one of her favorite cafes, Jardin du Nicola, and the man she saw sitting at the table in the corner made her stop breathing. He'd have a heart as big as a sunset, she knew right away.

Bertha hurried to him.

"Hi, it's me, I'm so happy you're here. You remember me?"

It had started raining outside the café and the air was thick with winds and clouds, most of the people had gone to bed because they had to go to work on the following day. She had to work on the following day, too. She had to finish translating a short story about a ballet dancer, but she felt she was about to write a wonderful poem, the best one in her Oostende.

"You remember what we did when we were together in Oostende?" she asked the man. His face was beautiful and his beer was Leff Brune, very dark and very sharp, exactly the way she liked it. "Do you remember the sand? We made the sun so small that you put it in my heart, and you said I was so quiet."

Bertha would like to go on telling him what they did in Oostende on the North Sea in winter, although the sand was cold and the waves were bigger than the sky and the water flooded the suspension bridge. She wanted to tell him his skin was lonely as a soft early autumn and his hands were the last warm day she'd have in her life.

"Yes, I remember," the man said suddenly. "I do remember very clearly. You were there with me. We kissed. But it was not in Oostende. No, it was not Oostende and it was not in Belgium. We were in the mountain. Do you remember the name of that mountain?"

He looked at Bertha his eyes bright and wonderful.

Bertha thought, "Now I'll disappoint him. I've never been to that mountain the way those guys were never in my Oostende."

"We were happy," the man went on. I remember clearly the warmth of your kiss, your smile. I've been so lonely. I didn't have anybody to talk to. Do you remember what you told me? I'll never forget it."

Bertha didn't know what to say.

"I said that I'd love a man that had a sunset in his heart," she said because that was what she'd always wanted to tell her man.

The stranger looked at her and smiled his eyes a sunny day after long winter of rain.

"I've been waiting so long for you," he said. "I didn't think you'd remember my name. It's so simple that everybody keeps on forgetting it."

Suddenly it stopped raining.

"Jake!" she said, her heart missing a beat.

"Yes, my name is Jake," he said his smile big, endless. "You remembered it!"

Bertha didn't know what to say.

Blue Grass

Maybe it was a trap. I always suspected foul play. I thought Val had planned it all, carefully, taking his time. Val was my cousin, and it was he that told me the water dissolved everything. It dissolved your shoes and your glasses, it dissolved the iron fenders of your car, and if you were not careful enough, it dissolved your fingers when you touched it. Yes, my cousin's fingers were gone after he dipped them in a jar of that water. His hand hadn't bled after that, he said. His fingers were all gone and his wrist looked like a big handle of a hammer. It didn't hurt, he added. It didn't itch. For a second he felt like water wanted to dissolve all of him, and that was all.

"It can't be true, Val," I told him.

"It is," he said.

Then he went to that spring many times hoping he could get a clue where his fingers had gone. Of course, I thought it was a crazy thing to do. He hurried there, to that narrow gorge where the spring was. He trudged all the way up to the naked hill so often that I started suspecting something was wrong. One evening I followed him, very quietly, very slowly, like a shadow of a bird. He should have noticed me, though. He was a bright guy, and he seemed to smell danger. He was a physicist. I was a physicist, too, and deep in my heart I knew the truth: he was a better scientist than me, an unfathomable, rich intellect, and that knowledge poisoned my peace. I tried to imitate him. I even tried to talk the way he did, calmly, thoughtfully, scratching my forehead from time to time.

When I learned about the water that dissolved everything my first impulse was to burst out laughing. It was impossible for any water to dissolve your fingers and your shoes and remain as transparent as a baby's tear. One more lie, I said to myself. Then he showed me the stump of his wrist that looked like a burnt potato and I thought he had lost his mind. He went to that spring in the gorge every morning and every evening of the week, and I thought he was in for another series of queer experiments. These, in the long run, earned him a prize, or at least a reputation of an odd, but dreadfully talented researcher. I lived on, my envy eating me, my jealousy scorching my brain. I envied him, even his disfigured hand.

One night, I followed him to that spring. You wouldn't believe what I saw. There was a bunch of women and men at the bottom of the gorge, and there was no blue grass sprouting from the rocks. Blue grass was everywhere in the Hole—only blue grass and no trees, no animals, no insects.

The Hole was the place of blue weeds which you could eat. You touched them to warm yourself if you were cold, and you slept very well if you pressed your body against the grassy wasteland. When it was dark, and in the Hole, it was often dark for no reason at all, the blue grass shone and it felt lively and pleasant everywhere. When you were sick, you covered yourself with that blue grass, and your sickness was gone. You could even make love to the grass, my colleagues told me, but I had never tried.

There was perfectly normal drinking water in the Hole. Looking at it, you wouldn't say it was different from the one that could dissolve your fingers. The normal water was blue during the day and evaporated at night, leaving beautiful dark blue patches of strong grass in its wake.

The narrow gorge where Val went left me spellbound. The grass there was puny and withered, and I took no interest in it. I concentrated on the spring, which resembled a puddle. It shone and gleamed, light blue, beautiful. I could see my cousin Val, his profile outlined against the steep walls of the gorge. I watched, hardly able to breathe. I needed to examine the place closely before I realized what had struck me. All the people sitting around the puddle had maimed or missing limbs. There was a girl who had lost her left hand; then I saw a fingerless guy, and a woman with her left foot gone. They all stood quietly, their faces anxious, waiting for something I couldn't see.

My first impulse was to go ask them what they were doing, then I noticed something that made me change my mind. My cousin was holding hands with a woman. Val, that cold fish, sat by the puddle and the woman stared at his face, smiling in the blue light of the grass. I wouldn't say she was pretty. Her face was narrow. After I glanced at it, I suddenly thought of the gorge. Her eyes looked soft and deeply black as if the dark patches of the grass were in them. There was something frightening in those eyes.

I had had many women and I knew when a woman's eyes looked so deep and frightened amidst the glowing grass. And I knew when a man's eyes were like a roar: the man was in love, something that fortunately had never happened to me. Love complicated things, women made scenes. I'd admit it was pleasant when they said you were their blue grass and their blue light, and I felt flattered when they said they'd do anything for me. At the end, they all ended up either screaming at you or imploring you not to go. I hated these scenarios. I'd rather have an emancipated girl of the type that didn't fall for pleading or sobbing. Love lasted a couple of minutes, and I found it unreasonable to put up with a woman longer than that.

Val's girl was tall and thin, dark and dark-haired or perhaps it was the light of the grass that made her look swarthy. Whatever the truth, she was not my type. Yet, she was Val's girl and that made her special. Val the physicist everyone admired. Val the researcher who sacrificed his fingers for the glorification of science. Science my foot!

There were nights when suspicions gnawed at my busy mind.

Science didn't attract me. Wasting my time in the lab made me sick at heart. Yet, I wanted to prove to my mother I was better than him. I wanted to prove her wrong when she pointed out ever since I was five, "Val had straight A's all through high school." Val was awarded a gold medal for his research in quantum physics. Val won the Guggenheim fellowship. Val became a full professor at twenty-nine, which I could never achieve.

Well, Val was holding hands with a plain woman who had lost three of her fingers—another sacrifice to the high altar of science, I suppose. I knew this type of women and I disliked them with all my heart. But she was Val's girl. Lying quietly in the warm glowing grass I knew what I'd do. I knew I'd have her on my blue lawn. I'd make her eyes roar and wait. I'd make her dream about me. I'd make her long to kiss my shadow. I was not a good researcher, yes. Well, I knew I wasn't even a mediocre researcher. I couldn't compare to the dust under Val's old textbooks, but I could turn a woman's eyes into a scream that followed me through the lawns of blue grass.

Speaking of lawns, there were no houses in the Hole. They were unnecessary. The grass was your house, it gave you warmth, light, and food; it gave you your baths in the morning when some blades of grass turned into blue water. The only buildings in the Hole were the laboratories, but they weren't necessary, either. The grass gave you what you wanted to know. You simply thought about it and you saw the answer in your dreams. The task of the researchers in the Hole was to study the blue grass, to analyze it, to explain why it turned into blue water and why the blue water was different from the transparent one—the special liquid which dissolved everything.

I didn't care much about research, why should I if the grass told me everything I wanted to know? I went to the labs in the rare cases when I took flowers to women who worked there. I didn't like women who pored over samples of blue grass. I knew they were conceited and thought too much of themselves. They made scenes.

I'd followed Val's girl for a week. I still didn't know her name. Perhaps the guard at the information desk could help me with that.

It was easier than I imagined. I gave the guard my identity card and my researcher's code. It was a perfectly natural thing to do, I'd done it many times when I filed a request for additional information on Val's girl, the lab associate I'd taken a fancy to. Dating was encouraged in the Hole. If you were eager to know a girl's name that meant you were interested and ready to devote precious minutes of your spare time to her. Our shrinks believed that activities of this kind boosted up the researchers' scientific endeavors. I was much inclined to dedicate my precious time to women, different ones every time. Come to think about it, my natural propensity for discreet dates with ladies of high academic achievements was evidence that I was one of the few powerful intellects selected to work in the Hole.

To be honest, my mind was far from being powerful. I hated hard work as much as I hated research. The longer I thought, the stronger my conviction became that I was selected to work in the Hole because of my irresistible charm. I loved good gossip, and I enjoyed learning little details about the guys and girls I knew. I wrote down beautiful descriptions of how the lassies I had been with behaved. I enjoyed perusing my writings in the quiet blue evenings, congratulating myself on being an astute observer of human behavior. I had noticed all the guys I knew were prone to exaggerating their virtues. All without exception, even Val, were open to flatteries, which I readily gave them.

To cut a long story short, I had numerous friends in all walks of their scientific careers and I had visited the blue grass lawns of almost all researchers in the Hole. The guard at the information desk of the laboratories was my friend, too. I had a beautiful description of him in my books. I had written down he was shy, over-credulous, and soft-hearted. I used this combination of adjectives to indicate that the person they qualified was far from being bright. This guy had fallen in love twice with the same redhead. He had been ditched twice and was still mooning over the redhead's photos despite the fact she'd sneaked out of his lawn without saying goodbye.

"Hi," I said, "I've seen a girl who works for the lab, a tall dark one, not too good looking. I hope you can give me her name. I'd appreciate it if you can tell me where her lawn is." Then I showed him the holographic picture of Val's girl I had taken as she climbed down the gorge with the peculiar blue spring. "I'd like to get to know that girl."

Then a strange thing happened. The guard's face contorted with emotion, and I had to wait until he pulled himself together.

"I don't know her," he said at last.

"Oh, my friend, come on," I said. "Tell me who she is."

The guy was silent, looking down at his desk. Perhaps he had fallen for her in the big silly way of his, or maybe he had seen the way she looked at Val, I couldn't tell.

"She's not even pretty," I said.

"I don't know her," he said stubbornly.

I looked at him closely, trying to work out why he was lying to me.

"Perhaps you are not allowed to tell me, "I said slowly. "Come on, I am your friend."

Beads of perspiration shone on his forehead. His white cheeks trembled.

"You *are* my friend," he said. "I know you are my only friend."

Strange why people thought I was a friend, very strange. I listened as they talked gibberish about their enormous plans, about their brilliant careers, and their girlfriends. I did the listening and offered them my generous compliments and praise. I'd concluded no one was impervious to blandishments. Men were so alone in their ambitions and careers. They rarely had companions in their isolated, well-arranged lives and anyone giving them admiration was their best friend. I'd written that down in my notebook of descriptions. Val was the perfect researcher, but his perfection, his achievements, were nothing if there was not a simple guy like me to extol and eulogize his scientific prowess.

"Look," said he.

He took off his blue laboratory gloves and showed me his left hand. His skin was white, his nails looked pink and well-shaped. It was an ordinary man's hand like any other I had seen. It was an ordinary hand that had no little finger.

"What's happened to your pinkie?" I asked.

It was a very quiet, clean room, and there were flowerpots with fine blue grass in them. In the laboratories, the researchers kept blue grass to kill the harmful microorganisms and purify the air. I noticed the grass was slowly turning light blue, a sign indicative of dangerously high levels of stress in the room. The grass was at work to alleviate George's anxiety. The beads of perspiration on his forehead slowly disappeared.

"I wanted to give them my whole hand," he blurted out. "But they didn't allow me. They didn't let the water have more of me."

"Let the water have more of you? What do you mean?" I repeated looking at him closely.

"They think I'm good-natured and they think I'm kind of honest so the spring should have a part of me in it." His face was red, and his fingers trembled.

"Did it hurt?" I asked softly trying to avoid his eyes. I wanted to know more. I wanted to know everything. I'd noticed that when I looked a guy in the eye he stopped talking. "Does it hurt now, George?"

"No," he denied vehemently. "I wanted ... I still want to give the planet more of myself, but they say I mustn't."

"Who are they?" I asked before I had time to think.

Suddenly George shook his head and stared at me.

"You are a senior researcher," he gasped. "All researchers, even the junior ones like me, were invited to the spring."

"I was invited, too," I lied.

The grass in the flowerpots turned almost white. George's face was red. There were beads of sweat on his cheeks and forehead.

"Then you should know who they are," he said slowly looking at me. I avoided his eyes. "Go away," he said suddenly.

"Wait, George, wait," I shouted, but he turned his back to me and ran to the white door at the back of the room.

"George!" I cried out. "If you don't come back I'll run to the spring. I will dip my hand into it."

Then there was a sweet smell in the air and I could speak no more. My legs were heavy, and my shoulders couldn't move. There was soft music, like an endless field of cool blue grass that healed my rancor, eased my anxiety, and killed my envy.

I had never been invited to that spring.

For a split second, I remembered the narrow gorge, its steep walls, and its even gray bottom. Then I sat on the floor, serene and smiling, staring at the flowerpots with the grass. For a moment, the grass was colorless. Then it slowly, very slowly started to turn greenish.

"You wanted to see me," a voice said amidst my serenity. I looked up and there she was, the girl with the narrow face that made me think of the gorge, the only woman with eyes so deep blue as if all the grass of the Hole was in them. She was Val's girl. Her face was not pretty. Plain women were easier to deal with, I knew that by experience. They didn't expect you to indulge their every whim, and their hearts softened immensely after you told them they looked attractive.

"You are very attractive," I said.

She blushed darkly and then repeated, "You wanted to see me."

Her eyes were calm, and I disliked them. They analyzed me and I left them unimpressed. I hated it when women were not impressed. I knew I was a handsome guy.

"I saw you at the spring in the gorge," I said. "And I know you've lost three of your fingers in the water."

She was silent, her eyes on my face.

"I know Val has lost his whole hand. His arm looks like a handle of a hammer," I said. "And George has lost his little finger."

She was silent. She was not even looking at me, and I couldn't stand that. Women should look at me when I speak to them. I was angry.

"I am a senior researcher, but I have not been invited to the spring," I told her. "Why?"

Her blue eyes stared at me calmly, as if I was a stone or a desk.

"You are not a researcher," she said, pronouncing the words clearly, without a trace of hesitation. There was a ring of finality in her voice when she added, "I expected you to come searching for me much sooner." Then she tried to smile. Her narrow face lit and the gorge was again there, in front of my eyes, its steep walls impenetrable and dark, dangerous, and beautiful.

Then I thought Val reminded me of something I had seen. Val with his rare smiles, his quiet reassuring words. Val resembled the vast plain in the Hole, enormous interminable land covered with blue grass that gave you all you wanted. The wasteland gave all people light and food, cured deathly diseases, and had answers to all sorts of questions.

"I want to ask you to my lawn," I told her. "You look beautiful to me."

"Stop it, please," she said. "You want me because I am Val's girlfriend."

"Can't you imagine for a moment a man could want you because of what you are?" I said.

"Listen," she breathed. "If a part of you dissolves in the water, the Hole will become like you, selfish, calculating, and mean."

I thought she was not all there.

"How come you know I'm selfish, calculating, and mean?" I said.

The grass in the flowerpots was almost white again. I was under stress and it was trying to cheer me up. I hoped my uneasiness didn't show, but the grass made it evident, and I hated its white glow.

"The women you abandoned underwent psychiatric treatment which I supervised," she said.

"And you concluded I was selfish and mean," I said.

"Yes," she answered. "You'd better leave the Hole of your own accord."

"Oh, come off it! I like it here. I like it very much."

"Think about it," she said. "We made the spring in the gorge. We give it our ability to feel. You don't have anything to give it."

I was suddenly angry.

"I don't care about the spring," I said. "I don't want the Hole to become a paradise for nitwits. The stupid and the lazy will be blessed there."

"People will recuperate from surgery here," she whispered. "The blue grass will be there to comfort the desperate and give hope to the sick.

"Now I get it," I told her. "You are transforming the Hole into a big hospital, and you hope you'll be rolling in money in no time."

"Please, go away," she said. "We will pay you as much as you want."

Then I calculated. They wanted me to go away so they'd have the whole thing and all profits to themselves.

"There used to be no blue grass in the Hole," she said. "When Val dipped his fingers in the spring, blue leaves sprouted in the plains. Then the spring dissolved George's finger and we discovered another thing. If the water takes a part of you, you simply cannot lie to anybody anymore," her voice trailed off.

"What happened when you dipped your finger in the spring?" I asked. "Men started falling in love with plain women?" I wasn't that interested in the expression on her face, although I was curious to see it. I thought she'd start shouting at me, but I was wrong.

I wanted to get an idea of how much money they'd wring out of that little measly Hole.

"Well, how much?" I asked firmly.

"You wouldn't understand," she said. "You've never loved anybody but yourself."

'We could discuss my love life at your earliest convenience," I said.

Some colleagues of mine had mentioned in my presence the blue grass could make love too, but I had never tried that. There were several lonely men and women in the Hole—that was true. Or maybe that was exactly what happened to the blue grass after Narrow Face dissolved her fingers in the spring? The grass learned to make love. Love my foot! How come that spring appeared in the gorge?

"To be honest with you, I don't like you at all," I said to Narrow Face. It was a rule with me to keep my likes and dislikes to myself, but I wanted to bite her head off.

She didn't flinch. I didn't like that.

"The women you met were very happy during their first week with you," she said.

"Not only during the first week," I said amused. "You should have learned by now that there was nothing more than a first week. Happiness is an expensive article of trade and I don't offer it free of charge."

It was then that she looked me in the eye.

"Long painful treatment followed that *first week*," she said evenly, and, it appeared to me, sadly. "None of the women you met have recovered. The blue grass couldn't help so we kept you on the planet. We hope you can help." She paused. I didn't know why I liked her silence. "Now we think it is hopeless."

Her narrow face looked gray, and her eyes were not that brash grassy blue I had seen the moment she entered the room.

"Please, don't touch the water in the spring," she said quietly. "We are afraid the blue grass will die if you do. You are everything the Hole is not."

I could smell her anxiety and it made me feel good. The grass in the flowerpots was colorless now.

"Then perhaps you'll tell me how much you'll give me to go away?" I said, looking at her and enjoying every second of the immense silence around us.

"I am not authorized to negotiate," she said at last. "I suggest we meet here tomorrow at the same time. Then we'll have an answer."

I looked at her narrow back as she walked to the door at the back of the room. I suddenly knew why Val had fallen for her. Her steps were beautiful. They were so quiet they felt like an echo of a long-forgotten song. Well, I didn't go in for songs. That odd spring and its transparent water attracted me.

Imagine there are no other places with a spring like that, I thought. Imagine you threw a snake into the water and the Hole turned into a biting killer desert? I'd never go away from you, Narrow Face. Don't even think about it.

After she was gone, I ran through the endless plain, trampling the blue grass underfoot. The broken grass was beautiful. It smelled sweet, and it sang the way the steps of Narrow Face had crooned. It felt as though someone by my side was very happy, a woman during her first week with me. The grass gave me everything I wanted, it gave me more than that, it gave me peace and quiet, it gave me even Narrow face, but I didn't want them.

I wanted the spring.

I wanted the transparent water that could transform my thoughts into power.

I reached the even ground surrounding the spring. Then the sense of happiness and quiet was gone and there were the steep walls of the gorge.

"Don't do that, please! Don't touch the spring!"

I heard the steps first. They sounded like an echo of a beautiful song I didn't remember too well. I saw Narrow Face descending the path. I was about to stop and talk to her, but then I thought of him. I thought of Val, my cousin, the brilliant researcher. My mother had always pointed out how superb he was and how worthless I looked by his side.

I rushed to the spring. It was so small and plain I could not believe my eyes.

"Don't do that," Narrow Face shouted.

Suddenly, I was very hot. I rolled up my sleeves and I dipped my right hand into the clear transparent water.

The calm. The bliss! It felt like the whole world admired me. It felt like no one was going to lie to me again and there was peace I wanted to share with all people I knew. It felt like I could make all sick children healthy again and it felt like they were smiling at me.

"No!" that was Narrow Face's voice. It came from afar and it drove away the smiles of the kids I had made strong again. I looked around me. The grass was changing color. It was big and strong. I had never seen grass so thick before. I touched it and I suddenly knew I would make heaps of money. I knew I'd sell things and steal things. I knew I'd be powerful. I knew all that, but suddenly I missed the faces of the people I could have made healthy again. I missed the hope in the children's eyes I had just made happy.

I missed the blue grass.

Then I saw her on that path.

"Narrow face," I whispered.

After you gave your arm to the spring you always told the truth.

"Narrow face, you are beautiful," I whispered.

There was grass everywhere around me. It shot up, it sprouted, and it grew on the naked rocks. It was motionless and luxuriant. It rustled like heaps and heaps of banknotes I'd have.

"Narrow Face, come back," I shouted. "I love you."

She was gone. She was gone and the grass was all over the place.

It was green. As I looked at it the grass bit me and my skin slowly burned.

Laura

Laura never haggled over the price of the brandy she bought. She took the bottle, threw the money on the table and that was all. The people in these parts lived on the brandy they sold her, survived like the grass-snakes, sticking to the stones and the brown soil that yielded only evil hot peppers and potatoes. Hawthorns, blackthorns, and damson trees throve on the wild rocky slopes and, if you picked their small fruits, you made that yellow brandy that Laura was interested in. The folks raised their children on the money from their demi-johns, on wild plums, and the sun. The moon didn't give birth to days but to yellow brandy, wild and wicked, smelling of parasol mushrooms and rattling with the noises ravens made as they spread their wings.

Laura didn't bargain with the guys from the village of Staro. They were skinflints and their shadows reeked of fights and unpaid debts. She drove her ramshackle van to Staro through the knee-deep mud and the holes in the dirt roads.

She hated all the villagers but knew she had to put up with one of them, Stoyko. He had two little sons, wild like eels, agile and taciturn, yet he regularly took Laura to one of the empty houses on the periphery of the village. Stoyko had a wife as well, a pale, silent shadow that climbed the hills, picking haws and sloes for the brandy. That woman sucked tomatoes out of the sand and planted cherry trees in between crags and rocks, stunted, undersized saplings that grew there despite the savage heat. Laura had seen her many times drag huge tin cans full of duck-weedy water to her cherry trees. There were some puddles, miserable remnants of the river, which didn't run dry in summer.

In summer, Stoyko took Laura to that derelict house; many of the houses remained ownerless if you didn't count the old dogs that outlived their masters. There, amidst the ancient rugs and bleached photographs of mustachioed men, women, and flocks of children, Laura and Stoyko made love. Laura didn't know what Stoyko did to make the men in shabby trousers sell her their brandy cheap. Perhaps it was his ill temper that at times scared her, or maybe they did it because he dug the graves for their deceased relatives for a very modest fee. In return for a loaf of white bread, Stoyko dug a most wonderful grave, deep and comfortable, and dead folks joined their maker without a hitch. Perhaps their maker was not very keen on that village, some suspected.

They had stones instead of land in their gardens, but then stones were useful, too. Snakes mated under them. The children here became rocks and snakes from an early age. They drank their fathers' brandy which smelled of ravens, clouds, and stolen pine trees. For fuel, men hewed the pines furtively at night. The plundered hillsides, denuded of trees, shone like bones and produced toadstools. Snakes slept under their flat heads; lizards, thick like ropes, ate them until unexpectedly the sky exploded and started dumping rains on the potato fields.

Rain after rain and no break for two months until the river was born again. It rushed, rumbling, sweeping roots and bushes, wrenching sand from beneath the sitting rooms of the houses. The water dragged along drowned snakes and lizards and Laura remembered it had mixed with the brandy in the demijohns. Then the river smelled of pines and ravens, the brandy was the color of dead snakes, but she and Stoyko were very happy in that ownerless house despite the downpour. Everything around them was wet and Laura wondered if the puddles on the floor were water or brandy. She had seen Stoyko's wife in the mud, erect like a lamppost under the rain, watching.

Laura chose Stoyko for two reasons: the thick brandy, and because most of the other villagers were old men who didn't look at her the way Stoyko did. At times, she thought of his sons. Last year they went to school by bus, then they had to walk, for petrol was too expensive. Children here were like the fish in the river that ran dry, a true rarity. Unlike the fish, the water snakes learned to live on dry land and mated with the real snakes. Thousands of them were born and swam in the rain. When Laura drove the brandy to Pernik, she smelled of pines, of mushrooms and snakes.

In the beginning, she sold it in the main square, squatted down behind a makeshift stall, an ancient table. She had pilfered it from an old house whose landlord was a feeble mutt. Laura managed to always push up the price, then checks started and inspectors wanted to see her permit, which she didn't have. She then rented a cellar from Nenko, a mechanic who could make a car out of an old vacuum cleaner if he wasn't too drunk. Laura paid him the rent in brandy but not the one that smelled of swelling rivers. She gave him a glass of the hogwash brew she bought from the gypsies in the village of Vladimir. These gypsies made brandy out of cabbage leaves and turnips, or maybe they used cinders to produce their concoction. One often had headaches and one's mug became blue after drinking it. Nenko's mug, however never became blue, he felt no pain and was quite comfortable with the Vladimir brew she gave him. He told her once, "I'd die for you." But he could not love her when he was drunk. He only made broken boneshakers good again.

Laura sold her brandy in thick opaque glasses she had pinched from the house of the old mutt. A disordered line of men, bluish in the face, formed down the flight of stairs to her cellar. The men downed the Vladimir brandy contentedly for she sold it dirt cheap. When Laura remained in the mechanic's cellar for a week, Stoyko arrived in Pernik to visit her. She could only guess how much he had squandered to reach Pernik. He rushed to her cellar and thundered, "Where's the other guy?"

He was spoiling for a fight with the men from the line because, in his view, Laura probably cheated on him. She locked and bolted the door then she made love to him while the guys waited humbly for her to open the cellar again. They desperately wanted their thirty-five cent glass of Vladimir. Stoyko could hardly bear them all the same.

"Let's run away to Spain," he told Laura. "We'll plant damson trees there, we'll distil brandy, and we'll make the Spaniards look blue in the face like us. Or, you come back home and stay with me."

In Pernik, there were no clients for the thick brandy with the sun and clouds in it, but Laura enjoyed its yellow presence behind her back. There was the river, the mushrooms and Stoyko's two sons in its amber depths. Laura had seen the boys write swear words on her van. Once, they punctured all its four tires with nails and the van lay down on the road like a dead cow. Then Laura watched the father thrash the kids with a stick he snapped off from the stunted cherry tree his wife had planted. It looked as if he had hit them with the tin-cans the scrawny woman had dragged in the scorching heat of July. The boys hadn't tried to evade the blows, their eyes fastened on their mother's face. When Stoyko was gone, they threw stones and cow dung at Laura. Strange, Laura was out of sorts because of that woman who didn't do anything but stick out from the ground like the goal in the empty football field. An open goal that nobody cared for, that was what that woman was. Laura felt sorry for her, but not so much as to give her a bill from the bundle she had in her pocket after she sold the Vladimir brandy.

She felt sorry because her own mother lived alone in one of the houses beneath the Black Peak. Her father had moved in with a young woman Laura liked and played backgammon with from time to time. Laura's mother was sparing of words, her face closed like a wall. Perhaps her father was right to move in with Darina. Darina, who smoked like a brick field, sang pop hits, jumbling up tunes and rhymes in a hot unbearable mess. She sold vegetables in the market square in Pernik and her mouth never ceased babbling even if she had a cigarette in it. Laura's father listened to her, smiling, happy that he could hear a human being speak. When his second wife shut up to light another cigarette, her father's face looked worried.

When Laura was little, her mother chased the boys away from their backyard. The girls were afraid of her, too, because of the wall she had instead of a face. If Laura wanted to kiss a boy she had to walk to the neighboring village. Rumors had it Laura's mother dabbled in black magic. All she had done was to buy a cheap plastic icon to which she prayed day and night, petitioning for her daughter to become rich. Laura's mother was taciturn, but her power of speech broke down completely when she found her husband with a woman, their neighbor of many years. The man had simply called in for a chat, but the woman's words had plunged into his heart and he had kissed her. Laura's mother lapsed into silence and neighbors said it was not an accident that toadstools sprouted up in her backyard, slugs infested her garden, and under the ground the moles were so many they ate even the rocks. It was only the brandy in her house that was good.

One day, Yani came to buy brandy from Laura's cellar. In fact, she came to know his name was Yani much later when he paid for a gallon of the sickening brew from Vladimir. He started drinking it mulishly, his back propped against the wall, tears welling up in his eyes. His face became blue, even his black eyes turned blue, and Laura feared he might breathe his last in her cellar.

"Why are you doing this?" Laura asked him, noticing that regardless of his livid complexion the young man was as handsome as an angel. He had dark hair and a face that appeared like a prayer to her, the face she had been dreaming of while her van got stuck in the mud of the dirt roads. She had seen that face while Stoyko groaned he'd do anything she wanted, forgetting it was raining, and that drowned grass-snakes floated down the river. Yani's dark drunk tears dripped into the cheap brew from Vladimir as Laura kissed him.

"She's gone," the lad muttered.

Laura asked him what his name was and he didn't know. Laura had been dreaming all her life that someone would forget his name because of her, but that never happened. Her own name was notorious in the whole district and when villagers saw her van, she knew they said, "The leech will be here again." Women substituted her name with other insulting words and Stoyko's wife was said to be seized by a fit beside the pot of soup she cooked if one of her sons mentioned Laura's name by mistake.

Laura took out the lad's wallet and his identity card told her his name was Yani. She kissed him again and slammed the door in the noses of the men who waited for her brandy in a quiet line. They were soft-spoken and one might presume they were in a church or waited in front of a surgeon's office. Sometimes Laura awarded a 'Vladimir' to the most tractable one among them. A Vladimir meant a free beer-bottle of the gypsy brew. The lucky man who got it swept the floor and smiled at Laura. She watched him closely, fearing he could pinch one of her precious opaque glasses. Although the door was locked, Yani didn't stop drinking and sobbing while Laura kissed him. He looked so beautiful, Laura made up her mind to give him a bottle of her true amber brandy. It was all August mornings, damsons and warm winds. The damson trees sucked life out of the crags and infused rocks into her brew. There was gold in the hills, and surely it squeezed its way into her demijohns.

Laura gave Yani the best of her amber treasure for she admired his chest so much. She had never been so impressed before, not even when her mother gave her a pair of green cords. Then the villagers wondered if it was really Laura or some pretty girl from Pernik who had lost her way and chased the wind amidst the snakes and lizards in their backyards. Laura's mother remained in her room, silent like the dead grass on the hills.

One day Laura discovered her mother had a mania for building a wall around her house. Her neighbors kept away from her even when she went to buy bread, so the woman started piling up rocks around her backyard. She dragged stones, thorns, and stray brambles that were welcomed by the lizards. When Laura came to see her mother, she lit up, if it was possible for a wall to light up. Her mother hugged her and Laura wondered how that woman survived there in the sun. The cherries had withered, the peppers had become dry like flint, and the moles had turned the garden into a wasteland of craters and molehills. Her mother had a nanny-goat named Hope, a bitch named Hope, too, an old TV set, and a calendar. Every time Laura visited her, the heap of stones around the house was larger, Laura wondered over her mother's sanity.

"How's your mother?" her father asked, taking a guilty look at the heat in her backyard. "They say she's off her head."

"She's okay," Laura said.

Once she found her mother talking to a young man whose face was much different from Yani's. That man's face was no icon and cried for no girl that was gone. That man was blond, colorless, and thin like the withered tomato branches behind the house. He constantly dug the garden and planted beans, looking more and more like the moles to which he talked in a soft, imploring voice. He spoke to Hope, the bitch, and to Hope, the nanny goat, and her mother listened, smiling. Her mother appeared happy she could hear a living thing speak. Then her mother asked the scraggly man to tell her fairy tales in the evening.

Laura was rendered speechless. She didn't think much of his tales, yet she started to suspect she fancied the man. She gave him some of her amber brandy, a teacup, and asked him to come and catch grass-snakes under the stones with her. People gossiped, said that her mother caught grass snakes and baked them to cure her silence and aching knees with their skins. The blond man took a gulp of yellow thunder of Laura's brandy and his transparent face became purple right away. "What did you do to him," her mother cried out, terrified.

That purple face told Laura the blond one was not a real man and had most probably visited her mother to have his body cured with grass snake's skin. Laura left the two of them alone. She stopped asking herself why that scrawny guy had crawled behind the pile of stones and thorns, surrounding her mother's backyard. Laura's mother had cured him for a month before his face healed and became again white and soft like a girl's. One evening, Laura found the two of them sitting in front of a bucket of milk. Hope, the bitch, sniffed at a heap of snake's raw meat. Hope, the nanny-goat, bleated softly. It was pouring rain and animals and people were in the sitting room.

It was autumn, the best time to buy brandy in these parts. So many toadstools had sprouted around the thorns and stones in her mother's backyard that Laura was scared. When she examined them carefully, she gasped. They all were edible mushrooms. The scrawny man and her mother drank milk and smiled at each other. That was so frightful and so amazing that Laura couldn't believe it. Some guys in the village said the man was a brandy merchant, but that was certainly not true. The only brandy merchant in the village was Laura.

"What's your name?" Laura asked the scrawny guy, but he didn't answer. He had forgotten what his name was and sat there, smiling at her mother. Rain spurted out of the torn sky, but the blond one didn't see it. He looked at her mother, not even telling her fairy tales. He looked at her and didn't know his name.

Yani, too, had forgotten his name because of a girl. After Laura locked the door of the cellar, she took him behind the only demijohn of yellow thunder. There she admired his magnificent face and loved him. He couldn't concentrate, though. He told her time and again about that girl. She was so beautiful that it stopped raining when she showed up. This made no difference to Laura. She loved him on the mat Stoyko had given her. Perhaps his wife had woven it years ago. Stoyko never forgot his name. He had grown wild and refused to drink the amber brandy. He was afraid he might fall asleep while he was with Laura. One day, after Laura had taken Yani to her amber-filled demijohn in the cellar, the rain stopped and someone knocked at the door. That had never happened before. No one was allowed to bang on Laura's door, not even Nenko, the mechanic she paid two Vladimir bottles a month. He drank his Vladimir, cleaned the cobwebs in the cellar, and swept the floor. Whoever he is, he'll pay through the nose, Laura thought and opened the door.

A girl stood before her, such a pretty girl that the men who waited in an unsteady line suddenly sobered. Laura had not seen such a beautiful woman before, although women from the hills of the grass snakes and damson trees were usually pretty. Even Stoyko's wife was pretty when she jutted out like a sword, watching them from the backyard of the house.

"Go away," Laura said to the girl. At that point, she saw Yani's face light up. Yani's face, as beautiful as an icon that Laura had just kissed, glowed and smiled. The girl smiled as well, she smiled so thinly that the brandy in the demijohns throbbed. Laura's mother and the blond, colorless man had smiled at each other like that by the bucket with the milk. Yani rushed to the girl.

"Yani," Laura shouted. "Yani!" but he had forgotten his name again.

When Laura drove back with the van to buy up the brandy in the village of Staro, she saw a thing that amazed her. Stoyko stood alone in the middle of his backyard under a big bleached umbrella. "She went away with the children," Stoyko said to her.

His house looked exactly like it did two years ago, a low, one-story building, its backyard swimming in the rain; no garden, just puddles and mud. The green tomatoes had rotted on their branches, decaying peppers, gray like the clouds, hung to the sodden ground. It wasn't necessary to plod their way to the house on the outskirts of the village. Laura moved in with Stoyko. His sons' school timetable was still glued to the wall; their old shoes and his wife's apron lay on the floor in the kitchen. On the first day, Stoyko collected the odds and ends and threw them out of the house. A new garbage heap had sprung up behind the rocks and branches Laura's mother had piled around her backyard. There, amidst the mushrooms that grew like mad, Stoyko dumped all that old junk. Stoyko and Laura didn't go out of the house for a whole week. One of the neighbors brought them food and drink from the village grocery store, ample supplies of bread, sausages, and cheese. Love didn't happen when one was hungry.

The neighbor took care of them diligently because Laura had given him a pail of the thunder brandy. The man would have hauled the whole town of Pernik to them for a much smaller demijohn. Stoyko, wild with the brandy and Laura, smiled in his sleep. But he didn't forget his name.

Laura bought up all the brandy from the villagers. She took the whole summer, the hills they had been tramping, their damsons, kernels and sloes. She bought the hours during which the men had strained their ears listening to the gurgling noises in the casks, waiting for the amber and thunder to trickle into the brandy still. She loaded up the van with the demijohns and was off to Nenko, the mechanic, who had already scoured and scrubbed the cellar for her. Its clean floor shone like a mirror, her regular clients had already fallen down the flight of stairs and waited for her, money in fists, ready for a Vladimir. When Laura drove back to the village of Staro, she saw a rusty chain and a padlock hanging on the front door of Stoyko's house. One of the windows had been boarded up. Behind it was the room where he had eaten a mountain of bread and sausages and had made love happen as often as the raindrops in the rainstorm.

"Stoyko," Laura shouted out. "Stoyko!"

Nobody answered her. The dog that had been hanging about the house while the neighbor took care of their food had vanished. A crumpled piece of paper was nailed to the wall. Some words were printed in pencil on the scrap. There were no commas, no full-stops, just enormous spaces, like toadstools, between the warped letters:

-k i d s a r e h u n g r y i a m w i t h
t h e m s t o y k o

The money Laura had made, the yellow rain, the rust of the chain on the door, weighed her down. She stood rigid, her lips stiff, her eyes cold and remote like the autumn wind.

Ice

Ice was everywhere—blue, gray, even black in the valleys. Ice was a part of my job, I had to calculate when avalanches would start and when the surface would crack, engulfing the aircraft, the traffic-control towers, the pilots and passengers, prisoners, soldiers and police officers in charge of the Hole's security. It was my responsibility to organize search and rescue teams to dig and delve in the ice for survivors. Usually, no one survived in the fathomless cracks of the ice in the Hole. I was the only survivor. I had graduated poetry writing from the University of Sofia, and I wasn't a brilliant student. I was among the worst students that had ever set foot in the University. A dirge one critic called downright sloppy doggerel, another expert in the trade proclaimed to be experimental and sophisticated verse. I reckoned poetry was a quiet shelter a young woman could call her profession while she ran no risk to be labeled slothful. My professors said I was a sheltered person, sensitive, too, and it seemed to them I could live well perfectly alone, so they wondered why my poetry was so weak.

I didn't have friends in my native town, my parents were divorced, and I grew up in a boarding house for children whose parents weren't so keen to take care of their offspring. There were no bad teachers and all the time I felt like a caring nurse was by my side. In fact, the boarding house was my loving grandma.

I was not a particularly industrious person and the bliss in the boarding house made me even more indolent. The other children thought my parents' divorce was a blessing for me. Your parents earned a one-way ticket to the boarding house for you, they said. I majored in poetry writing because it was the easiest thing in the world. You didn't need to study much. These days no one really wanted poetry. Some crazy foundations paid you to go and study how to produce rhymes, concoct metaphors, and spew similes about a fact as simple as breaking with your boyfriend.

I was good at breaking with my boyfriends. I knew very well I had no literary talent at all. Art left me perfectly unperturbed. Unfortunately, I hated natural sciences. I guessed I had to work somewhere like everybody else, and the diploma of a poetess, or shall I put it an expert in poetry, would at least secure a position of a tourist guide in the Hole. For me, the Hole, the ice place, had become a hit among the tourist destinations. It was the most fashionable thing to get married amidst the ugly mountains and gorges of ice. The fools believed their marriage would be spotless if they tied the knot on the black glacier crescents of the Twin Hills, an abhorrent canyon near my office which was a small, gloomy place, dug out in a hill of black ice.

I was one of the passengers on the list of Flight S123 from Sofia, my totally uninteresting native town. I flew to Twin Hills in the Hole, the romantic nook young fools rushed to get married in. I had broken with four boyfriends so far, and I abandoned my love number five without batting an eyelid. I didn't tell him I wouldn't return to the flat we rented in a cheap suburb. I said I was going to buy a packet of dried dill for the soup I was cooking for him. I left the water and the meat boiling on the cooking stove.

"Hey," he said. "Take more money and buy a bar of chocolate for me."

I guessed he was disappointed he didn't get his chocolate. I didn't make the dill soup, either. I took Flight S123 to the Hole instead. I had signed a contract and I had to become the poet laureate who would write love hymns for the young nitwits that married on the Twin Hills.

The ice surface cracked when we landed on the old runway. The bad thing about the Hole was you never knew when the ice would break. It could open under your feet even though a minute before the black frozen wasteland was as immobile as a dead man.

I was the only survivor among the fifty-seven passengers. The crew, a happily married couple, was never found in the ice. The search and rescue team had found me frozen, my arms, legs, and ribs broken, their captain said. It was a wonder I hadn't died, the doctors exclaimed. No one could live so long without food and clothes in the Hole. The ice seemed to like you, the captain said. The search and rescue guys told me I was on top of a jagged icy outcrop. The other passengers were torn to frozen pieces in pools of frozen blood. I was the only one that had remained whole, not alive and kicking, but whole. It is impossible, it just couldn't happen, the doctors said. It's a wonder you are still alive.

It turned out I had a talent. I could predict when the ice would crack. I didn't know how it happened. I often thought about the guy I left in my shabby Sofia flat waiting for his bar of chocolate, and I felt like making love to him. Then the ice cracked. It just did. Even the slightest hint I wanted that guy made the ice toss and split. My boyfriend was a knowledgeable and peaceful sissy who constantly said he loved me. All my previous boyfriends used to say that, and it was a sign the time was ripe. I had to leave. Dad used to declare he loved mom, then he walked away on her and she landed in a psychiatric ward. Love was something dark and deleterious. The only good thing about love was its absence from my life. Making love was a different thing.

I thought about it, and I saw the guy waiting for his bar of chocolate. The ice cracked. The expert teams established the depth and width of the chasm using complex electronic equipment. I started warning the experts that the ice would kick and split and they canceled the flights.

Gradually, my reputation of a unique talent who had a particular feeling for the Hole's killing ice turned into a legend. The love hymns I composed were of a shamefully inferior quality, but young couples paid fortunes to have me dedicate a lyric song to their wedding day. I was called the ice queen, the mistress of ice, Lady Sovereign of Survival, and many other idiotic things I hated to repeat. I stood and stared at the ice, and that was what I did all day long. I hated the poems I wrote. They were flat, dumb, and completely lacking in inspiration. It was not necessary even to be vigilant to know when the ice would hit. If I had an erotic dream, I knew that the surface of the Hole would rent and lacerate its icy skin. The flights to the Hole were canceled, human lives were saved, and the citizens of the drab town of Sofia built an edifice, a palace of culture, they named after me. The Mayor invited me to come and deliver a speech on the day of its inauguration, an honor I declined. It was not so much the absence of vanity that made me shut up. I had to rise to the occasion and write a poem about Sofia, a thing I hated to do.

Another component was added to the legend woven around my name: my phenomenal modesty. Modesty my foot! I was the most vainglorious person in the world. I wished my father twisted and turned in his bed after he heard about me. I wished my mother writhed and squirmed. After she remarried she never phoned or asked how I was doing in the boarding house, that bland moronic educational institution.

The Hole got on my nerves. I was the guardian of its rifts and the icy precipices. I hated to be a guardian. Sometimes I wanted my boyfriend so much that the ice in the Hole cracked and quaked. Once I enticed a young man away from his fiancée. You couldn't imagine how she screamed and hollered and cried. Anyway, the search and rescue team found me almost dead, both my arms broken. I lay in a frozen lake of blood. They could not find the guy who had been with me.

"It's a miracle you survived," the doctor who examined me told me later. "It all seems impossible, but maybe the ice loves you."

I hated the glaciers, and the menacing height of the icy mountains gave me the creeps. I could feel more sharply than before, the Hole's surface kicked and cracked, and I constantly thought of the soup I had left on the cooking stove. I dreamed about my boyfriend. All the flights to the Hole were canceled. I lived in a fury of memories and blurred visions. In my sleep, I talked to him, and I dreamt I came back to the shabby apartment in Sofia. It was a nightmare; I was the only human being in the Hole. I noticed the color of the icy wasteland around me had changed. It became black everywhere. No more honeymoon flights to the Hole were announced, and no more planes landed on the airfield. I dreamt of the shabby apartment, I saw the bar of chocolate I never bought for my boyfriend. He was constantly before my eyes. His skin was smooth and sparkling. I loved it.

The ice broke and whined. Mountains of ice collapsed, whirred, buzzed, and pealed. The whole planet split and writhed, the hills tumbled and shattered. Fountains of black ice spurted from the gorges as I lay exhausted, unable to think of my boyfriend anymore. The four planes that came to extricate me from the freezing nightmare were engulfed by the gray abysses of crackling ice. The remote-controlled shuttles which brought food for me landed unscathed.

What happens in the Hole should be impossible, I read in the messages I received from the University of Sofia. The Hole wants *you*. It wants nobody else. Try to describe how you feel, what you think about when the ice breaks. Of course, I didn't tell them I saw Slav naked. I called all my boyfriends *Slav*. It was a name I hated. My father's name was Slav.

Do you see any connection between your actions and the *rebellion* of the ice in the Hole? I was not an idiot to tell them about it. I had my pride. I was an expert in poetry, a poor expert, it was true. But I was a great ice expert.

One day the shuttle brought me some disgusting yellow cake to eat, a large baking tin of yellowish rubbish. I hated cakes. In the boarding house, they always gave us cakes for breakfast, cakes on Christmas, and cakes on Mother's Day, too. I was alone in my office with the ugly lump of hard-baked dough. The walls of the room were all transparent, of course, and I had the feeling nothing separated me from the black booming ice. It felt like my skin cracked. I was hungry and I had nothing else to eat, so I ate the sinister looking cake.

I am convinced that even the most brilliant student in my poetry class—I hear he became quite famous for his *Snake Ballads* series—couldn't describe truly and fully the bliss and pleasure I enjoyed that evening. It all felt so real I couldn't breathe.

I was in my old apartment in Sofia. There was no ice there, it was a spring day. I never liked spring. It was wet and windy and the blossoms of the trees made me allergic and sour. The apartment was a sorry sight, the faded wallpapers, the greasy staircase, the smell of mold: all looked and felt the same. The man who lived in my flat was not Slav. He looked very confused when he saw me standing at the front door.

"You look like her," he stammered. "You look like her. Is it some trick?"

"Can I come in?" I asked. "I'll explain everything to you."

I didn't utter a word, though, I kissed him instead. He was astounded.

"Slav," I said.

We made love. It was too warm and too wet in the room, but I didn't care. I was sorry I was a third-rate poet, and I couldn't write a eulogy to his hands, a ballad for his mouth, an ode to his flat stomach, a hymn to every square inch of his wonderful skin. It was such a vivid hallucination I wished it would last forever. I kissed and kissed him. I loved him and my hunger left him dry and exhausted, smiling happily in the moist, smelly air. Was it the yellow cake that gave me that happiness? No doubt, it had some drug in it. What a fool I was. I should have kept a piece of it for the next time.

"Slav," I said. "I hate your name, but I love you."

"I'm not Slav. You look like the girl in the Hole. The famous poetess who saves people in the ice," he whispered.

"Slav, I'm hungry," I said.

He brought a jar of yellow honey. There was a label *Sunflower Honey from Sofia* on it and a picture of a sunlit field covered with yellow blazing sunflowers. I knew sunflower honey was the cheapest thing one could buy from the local supermarket. I kissed Slav. My hallucination and his lips tasted sweet.

I opened the jar.

Then I was again in my office with the transparent walls, amidst the black wasteland of dead ice.

"Slav," I shouted.

For a flitting moment, I saw him, I heard him say I was the most beautiful girl he'd ever seen. Then the black ice cracked so powerfully that the walls of my office shook and my bed shattered into uncanny pieces on the floor. There were rifts, fissures, crevices everywhere around me, all gaping black in the thick jumping ice. The Hole roared and shuddered triumphantly, closing in on all sides around me. It felt like making love. It was dreadful and it was fabulous.

Enormous edgy fragments of ice pushed their way into my office. The Hole had come for me.

Then I saw something on the table that made me freeze in my tracks. There was a jar and the label on it read *Sunflower Honey from Sofia*.

The ice that touched my skin was smooth and warm like Slav's hands.

Vassa

Vassa didn't need more time to mull it over again. Each time when her husband was drunk he collapsed on the pillow, face down, heavy, immobile, like dead. Then she dreamt about it, her worst fears making her freeze in her tracks. Her dreams brought her bruises, thick and black, all over her body. Whenever the pain grew purple, Vassa smeared blood from her cracked lips on the edge of the drab sink and stared blankly at it.

At the risk of being beaten black and blue by Meto, she had stolen money from the pockets of his trousers and had bought pencils. She had broken them in two and then had sharpened the pieces at both ends. Now she had four pencils. It had cost her ages of wariness, she was afraid both of Meto and of her son and she usually sharpened the pencils sticking her hands in the oven of the electric cooker. They had to be neither too long nor too short, so she sharpened them at night as well, but that meant wasting electricity and that, in its turn, meant more bruises. She was ready now.

Meto woke up on edge, shaky. He hadn't drunk last night and wondered why his mouth tasted bitter like death. The woman by his side slept like a log, his own wife. She was uglier than hell, her face, although not too old yet, looked puffy, minced meat stuffed in the plastic bag of his hatred. That woman dragged him to the gutter, to squalor, and poverty. Suddenly, he wanted to crash his fist into her head thinking of the sound of her skull creaking under the knuckles of his fingers. He could only guess why she had squeezed like a worm on the bed beside him. He had told her he didn't want to see her face anymore, didn't want that nasty ugly woman, but she had crept under his blanket just to spite him. The thought of how she'd scream made him stir in bed. He grabbed at her hair, clenched his fist and pulled. The woman groaned, she had not woken completely and her body shook. Meto saw her hands, gnarled, with distorted fingers and swollen cracked skin. Her legs, in fact, he could see only her feet, shook, too. That exasperated him.

Vassa had anticipated that. She didn't shriek. She had four pencils sharpened at both ends. The pain became nasty and she let out a sharp sound, a quiet intense scream. He reached out his hand and grabbed her hair again.

"No," she whimpered. "No."

A wisp of her hair remained in his fingers, black, thick hairs that made him mad. He gripped her head with both hands and pressed her to his crotch. It was not necessary for him to speak. She knew what she had to do and started doing it, her emaciated body convulsing, her hands with brown patches on them, with disfigured fingernails, her dirty heels shaking. Meto squeezed his fists into a ball and hit her head. Not right away, maybe several seconds later, her flesh sagged, her head drooped, her arms hung like old moldy firewood.

But she had prepared the four pencils very diligently; she had been working on them for months, dreaming. If she had not been so scared Meto or her son would catch her, she would have polished them with tears but the two of them could not stand the sight of her sobbing.

He hadn't killed her, he was sure of it. He had hit her many times and occasionally her nose bled, but now there was no blood in sight. That woman was his grave. Meto pushed her out of his bed, the bitter taste in his mouth erupting into scorching heat. He could discern her clothes—tattered skirts and blouses she had bought from the sleazy holes selling second-hand junk in the basements of the blocks of flats. At first, he felt like hurling all the rags out of the front door of the flat, but that would cost him a lot of effort.

Vassa was clever, she had thought of everything. No, she'd dreamt it all and her brain, dry and racked with pain, had seen all details. She could stick it out. She had prepared his pillow. Very cautiously, she had ripped open one of the seams and then, even more cautiously, praying to Virgin Mary for help, she had arranged the four pencils, sharp at both ends, in two vertical lines, an inch of soft dirty duck down between them. After that, she had placed the dusty feathers back carefully wrapping up each pencil. She had stroked Meto's pillow saying a prayer for each little sharp pencil. She was ready.

Meto had warned her not to lie on his bed. He had said the skin of her face made him sick and he could not stand her smell. He had made it clear he wanted her to cook his lunches and keep his clothes clean. Her son had said the same thing. It was living hell since the iron cistern smashed her leg in the shoe factory. She couldn't earn a cent, she only ate his food, his money. He threw her clothes out of the front door, his anger flaring up, slamming on his temples. He grabbed an object that came his way. It was an empty saucepan. He stumbled over it in the corridor and flung it through the open door, hoping it had hit her. The rattling sound echoed in all the rooms of the flat, but it didn't erase the bitter taste from his tongue.

He looked around the place perfectly sure he was in control of the situation. The neighbors had long ago given up poking their noses in his business; they already knew him well enough. Perhaps some of them looked through the peepholes but he didn't give a damn about it. They could do whatever they pleased.

Coming back to the bedroom Meto saw his son—a towering shadow in front of the door to the loo. The boy was tall and big, with long tousled hair. The teenager didn't budge, just stood, staring into space, like a lump of earth, a bottle of beer in hand, his back pressing the wall. Meto had woken him up, too. He watched as the boy took a swig. He was drinking the beer he had bought on his father's money. That pissed Meto off, but the boy was almost as thick and tall as him.

Meto peeped into the bedroom and saw the vixen still lying on the floor, her blotchy face buried in the old worn-out carpet. He felt like clobbering her, but she'd smear her blood on him and her blood smelled of her miserable life.

After he beat her, he fell onto his bed his face down to his pillow. She knew that for sure, it had happened so many times before. Nothing else could happen now, nothing else. She had prayed for it. He trudged past her and she hoped he'd walk away, but he stopped and kicked her. His foot sank into her chest. Boats and stars swam before her eyes, perhaps the Virgin Mary had come to take her away from here, or perhaps the black scarf of death was over her shoulders. No, she had to wait a minute. She had placed the feathers so carefully, wrapping up the pencils. The boats came closer and closer to her eyes, her breast hurt, and perhaps she had a broken rib again. Everything around her was still and quiet. What a pity she had wasted ages sharpening the pencils in the electric oven. Her efforts were in vain.

Suddenly, a wild roar split the walls of the bedroom.

Granite

Shon didn't have enough money. All his friends had forgotten him. He couldn't pay his sex tax and that meant that he could no longer be a man. He'd be processed into a stone, and he knew he'd be deaf and blind dust. Each particle of the dust he would turn into would be listening to her steps, Eya. How could he forget her? He'd been a stone several times for her.

Her family would never agree to pay his sex tax. They didn't want him around. They were heaps of brown stones around her and he had to climb and crawl to surmount them. He had to endure to reach her. They were endless hard sharp crags closing in on him, encircling Eya. When he finally managed to pay his tax, her father told him she had been processed into sand or a heap of stones. Shon went looking for her. How could he be sure she was the gray rock jutting like a knife into the sky? He believed he'd know, he'd been dust, lowly powder without form of its own, and he'd been a rock, so he knew, a rock would recognize if another rock was Eya.

She used to be a small island lost in the sea, then she was a dune. She was a hillock of sand and he was the wind in the night that touched it gently, very carefully. He loved her so much he wanted to be dust all his days without her. Shon had been sandstone and granite. He'd been patient. He'd been mud. And he had been a digger for years and years. Diggers were the sexless workers who cut the stones and carried the bags of sand with which other diggers built houses. He had been a stone and a bag of sand and other diggers had built a house with him. He mixed with other stones and he couldn't pay his sex tax to become a man. He had remained a wall of a house forever, rubble in the base of a mausoleum, a tile on its roof, a chimney dead with smoke. He could not become a man until the house crumbled and the roof disintegrated, and the chimney melted away.

The diggers were losers, the despicable riff-raff that lived to grab money. They were happy when they stole small change or killed other diggers for small change. They were no men or women; they were bad eggs that had no embryos in them. After ages of building houses and making roads, they could finally pay to be men or women for a day. Shon knew very well what it felt like to be a digger. He had built a garden amidst a desert for a newlywed couple. He watched as they kissed and he was there while they made love. His task was to bring them water and food. They liked his docility and paid him well.

Even while he was a digger he never forgot. He didn't know where Eya was. He hoped she was not a digger like him. He hoped he could earn enough to buy her off, to pay her sex tax. Her parents could pay any price and she could remain a girl all her life. Her parents could find a different man for her every time she was a woman, but Eya ….

Shon remembered. "You are my bread and you are my hunger," she had said. "I don't want anybody else. I'd rather be a digger all my life or a house that will never collapse if you are not with me."

Shon didn't want any other girl. He could afford to be a man an hour every year. There would be women for him. He could find a sweetheart and she'd love him. Being a woman was a short-lived bliss and every second was a treasure. It was a common sight to see a man caressing a piece of stone. His woman had no more money to pay her sex tax and her time as a girl had passed. Sometimes a woman held a pebble in her hand; that was the man she had kissed a minute before.

Shon knew what happened after the kiss. Women threw the pebbles away and rushed to find other men. Every second counted. Every heartbeat was rewarding. Men got rid of the stones that had been the love of their days. No one wasted time.

Eya was in his dreams. On the day he was a man, one short winter day in the endless year, he didn't look for another girl. He wanted Eya. "You are my shore and my infinity," Eya had said. Eya, his Eya.

"He's sick," the diggers said. "He's deranged. He's a stone that has crumbled the wrong way." But Shon was not a stone that had crumbled the wrong way. He hoped Eya was a pebble he could press to his heart.

"I'll pay the digger to carve your name on me, after he processes me into a stone, Shon," she had said. "And you'll know where I am. You'll find me."

"Your parents won't let you be a stone. They'll find someone for you."

"No," she said. "I will not be a woman for anybody else!"

He couldn't find her.

He'd been an outcrop of granite for all eternity before he made enough money to become a man again. He paid a digger to carve her name on the gray rough rock he had turned into. It cost him all he had earned while he was sand, and what he had saved up while he was dust and mud. The digger that had carved Eya's name on him could afford to remain a man for an interminable week on Shon's money.

Shon waited. He was a granite block. Winds hit him and the mist slept on him making his surface slippery and freezing cold. Birds perched on him and moss grew on him, destroying his crystals. Shon made money by slowly dying. He hoped the moss had not covered Eya's name. He prayed it remained cut deep and sharp into him.

One day Eya came. She touched the moss that grew on his surface. She dug carefully, very slowly the mist that enveloped him. She cleared the leaves of the trees that had been falling onto him for years. "Shon," she said. "Dearest Shon!"

A stone cannot feel, Shon had been told that many times. A stone is dead. A stone cannot love the summers and the winds. Shon knew all that. But that wasn't true. There she was, his Eya. *You are my bread and my hunger. You are my eyes. You are my mist, and my birds, Eya.* He understood her words. He could feel her touch. He had been a sexless digger so long, and he had loved her. He had been dust, the storms had scattered him all over the world, and he'd loved her. He had been a road of stones that her parents destroyed, and he'd loved her.

Something was happening. His surface broke. Deep crevices cut through his cold depth, the moss which grew on him caught fire. He had paid that digger to carve Eya's name on him. Now, her name was no more. His crystals creaked and shrieked, his granite depth writhed and shook. There was no more strength in him. He was not a stone anymore. He was not sand, not even dust. He didn't know what was happening to him. Then he heard her voice.

"Look!"

"Yes, you were right, my child."

That was her father speaking. Shon could understand. He recognized the man by his firm touch. Shon had been a stone and her father had kicked him and pushed him hundreds of times.

"Look at it. What a beautiful ruby," another voice said, a man Shon had never seen before. "You wouldn't imagine cheap granite could make such a splendid ruby."

"Oh, they all do, James," her father said. "The trick is to make them fall in love."

"My fiancée is very good at that," said the man Shon had never seen. "You are unbelievable, Eya. Congratulations."

"Thank you, James."

There were no winds and no mist. Shon was not a man and had no heart. Something much more powerful than a heart broke in him.

"Let's wrench that beautiful ruby from this rubbish heap," her father said.

"That's the best gem in your collection, dear," the man she called James remarked as he carefully placed Shon in a box. A dozen of other smaller rubies sparkled momentarily under the thick lid.

The thing that was more powerful than a heart screamed deep inside Shon, *You are my bread and my hunger. You are my coast and my infinity.* Perhaps Eya didn't know that a ruby was a stone that would live longer than the wind.

Nikola and the Crocuses

He could not look at the dog's light brown eyes. It started to rain. "Come on," Ivan said. The dog slowly followed him and climbed up on the backseat of the bone-shaker. Jivil was a peculiar mutt, yellowish-orange like a crocus, but so feeble and aged that he could hardly stand in front of his kennel. Jivil used to be a good guard of Ivan's house but there was no life in the old dog anymore. When thieves once stole some instruments from the backyard, Ivan bought a new dog—white with brown and black spots on his back. There were no crocuses and no rains in him. The newcomer had sharp teeth, malice, and youth, and no burglar could lift anything from the backyard.

"Come on," Ivan repeated.

Ivan's car was a ramshackle Ford, third or fourth hand. He hated it when his friends saw him drive it. He imagined he looked like the old Jivil, his fur thinning at the back, rains in his eyes, death stalking behind the clouds.

Ivan was forty-seven when his wife gave birth to a third child, a boy, after his two daughters had grown and had children of their own. The boy, a dot of a child with red hair, was called Nikola after his mother Nika. While Nika did the housework, the boy and Jivil talked above the dog's empty bowl, a black eye, staring angrily at the sky.

The old Ford, which lacked any enthusiasm whatsoever, whirred and wheezed to the forest. Ivan knew he had to go a long way. Not only to the village of Bosnek but much further, behind the springs of the Struma River, into the wilderness where even wolves would lose their way. The man and the Ford plodded on while the dog barked at the road from time to time. "Shut up, Jivil," Ivan muttered. Perhaps Jivil was deceiving himself that his master was again taking him hunting despite his scuffed coat. The dog constantly raised his nose to the windshield.

Ivan had risen early in the morning on purpose so Nikola couldn't see him.

Nikola was a quiet comma which separated the days of Ivan's life and made his home complete and alive. Even Ivan's back, that he had injured in Italy, did not hurt so much when Nikola was around. There was no place in the world where his thoughts could go if Nikola was not there.

There were dozens and dozens of holes in front of his Ford. Not a road, but a guillotine for the poor car which positively had driven more interesting folks in its heyday; Italians, and then some Turks from whom Ivan bought it. The guys just happened to pass through Pernik and were grateful they finally got rid of their rusty rattle-trap.

Ivan was a teacher in Bulgarian literature but there were not enough students in town, so he taught at the school for mentally retarded children. His students had difficulties remembering things. His wife was a teacher in physics, but there were no vacancies and she made tapestry cushions and prepared to go and work at a hotel in Greece. Ivan couldn't feed an old dog at home. He couldn't leave him to starve, either.

The road before Ivan vanished altogether, then the track disappeared and only the hill was left.

"Come on," Ivan told the dog, but even before he had finished speaking the orange pelt was jumping through the bushes. Ivan took out a plastic bag. There were bones and stale bread that he and his wife had been collecting for a week. Ivan had added a piece of cheap sausage. He had hidden it yesterday night from his dinner. He could do that much for Jivil.

He and his wife had carefully taken away the cubes of bacon from the sausage for Nikola. One never knew what sort of bacon they put in that cheap sausage. Ivan emptied the plastic bag with the bones and the shriveled piece of cheap sausage. The dog looked at him gratefully and bayed deeply, the way he did when Nikola took him for a walk to the hill. That hill was the end of the town of Pernik and the beginning of the disused colliery in which there were no coals. There were only rusty rails and old goods wagons in which snakes and spiders bred. The boy and the dog went about the deep ruts and Ivan was worried sick they could collapse in some old shaft.

"Eat this," he said to the dog. When Jivil licked his hand the man didn't pat him on the head as usual. He withdrew guiltily, made for the car without turning back, started the engine and drove along the dirt road, through the holes, each one a grave for the ancient bone-shaker the Turks had gotten rid of.

The dog looked around confused, left the bones, and forgot even the shriveled piece of cheap sausage which Ivan had kept for him from his dinner. His barking—deep, long and loud—mixed with the autumn leaves. Ivan could hear it but didn't turn back for he didn't want to see the dog's back with the fur falling off. He couldn't look at the eyes in which it constantly rained and death waited for the last autumn day.

The dog ran after the car. Finally, he lost the game, yet made it to the asphalt road, crouched down beside it, and set up a quiet deep-toned howl. Ivan drove quickly, as quickly as his old tub of a car could. He hated the rear-view mirror, although now it didn't reflect the dog, but the roofs of the village of Bosnek. Ivan kept on seeing rain even though it had stopped raining. It had stopped raining long ago. He parked his car in front of the school for mentally retarded children where the students studied very slowly. He was on duty during the night. He was in charge of all these kids, but he was not sure he could teach them any good at all.

In the afternoon, he went home to his house where the town of Pernik ended and the empty colliery began. The railroad reached almost to the door to his backyard. On the curb, in front of the house, Nikola, the red-haired comma that separated all sentences in Ivan's heart, waited. Although it was autumn, his son sat on the stone and played with the frayed leash on which they kept Jivil. The boy had put half a piece of the cheap sausage in the black dog's bowl, an old piece of sausage from which someone had carefully taken away all cubes of bacon. Nikola stood up from the curb—a mite, a little round stone, hurled near the house.

"Where is the—" he began, but his father cut him short.

"Listen, I'm in a hurry. I have to help your mother."

The red-haired boy bent his head, a reddish kite that had by chance tumbled in their backyard. He rolled the leash into a ball and thrust it under his shirt.

At noon, the boy fell sick. His mother left the tapestry cushions she was weaving. His grandmother, a small woman who lived in the neighboring borough and smiled easily, came. She brought honey and dried linden blossoms to kill the high temperature. The boy didn't say anything, just listened to her, as quiet as a crocus in his bed in the kitchen where it was warm. He easily swallowed the pills his mother gave him. On the following day, the rain stopped, the wind came from the empty colliery smelling of old wagons and spiders, the street behind the window was full of autumn. The boy was again running a temperature and the doctor made up his mind to put him on antibiotics.

Ivan came back from school. The children there, although they had difficulties remembering and studying things, had made greeting cards for their teacher's red-haired boy. There were smiling kids in these cards and a couple of scribbled words, "Get well, Nicko."

Nikola, too small for his heavy grand name, lay in his bed in the warm kitchen and spoke to the TV that was on, or perhaps he was talking in his sleep. Ivan brought him another dog—a brownish-black thing that he kept on Jivil's leash. The boy tried hard to smile and gave up somewhere halfway through it. His mother sat by his side with a bottle of medicine and other pills.

It was cold and rainy, the red roofs of the houses thawed in the clouds, the wind hid somewhere, and Ivan didn't know what else he could bring his son. It was quiet and gray and his boy probably lay in his bed in the kitchen. Ivan was walking slowly toward the end of Pernik, to the hill from which the autumn was to go away. It was impossibly quiet. The railroad of the colliery ended abruptly on this street, and his backyard began. If only Jivil could come back, but he had driven him far from here, too far. Even the Struma River was not there. There were no springs either, only wilderness. He'd do everything for his boy. There was nothing to be done. Ivan didn't feel like looking up. When he finally did, he couldn't believe his eyes.

Crouched by the curb, a boy and a dog sat side by side on the stone. Jivil and Nikola, both of them yellowish-red, the kid small, his hair very short, the dog's fur falling off from his back, sat together, two crocuses that had unexpectedly grown by the railroad of the colliery.

Zina

Her husband had to look for a job in Spain, so on Monday, he, together with dozens of men like him, dressed in denim pants and thick padded coats, boarded a bus to Madrid. Zina and he fought in the evening, but in the morning, she gave him a little money before he left, lying to him it was everything she had. Before he closed the door, Zina spoke to him about the debts he had left her. She had to live on less money per month than the price of a pair of cheap shoes.

Yes, the idiot had left a mountain of debts in his wake. Six buddies of his knocked at the door of her apartment an hour after he had left. The biggest of the men, their neighbor Stoyan, wanted Zina's fridge and TV. He couldn't wait, he pointed out. He wanted his money back. He would not wait a minute more.

"I don't have a penny," Zina said.

"No way," Stoyan barked. "I'll come tomorrow. You'd better give my money back."

Zina had looked forward to the minute when there would be no one else in her apartment. She was going to have the time of her life, would be free from her husband's sour face, and her sons' bitter fights over small change. It turned out Zina had jumped from the frying pan. Her husband's friends wanted their money from her. She didn't have a penny to bless herself with, she told them. Other men, gruff and sour, came, declaring he owed them two grand. She had to settle all accounts, this went without saying, they pointed out.

Her sons were like their father, blabbermouths, finding no decent jobs. Both were constantly broke so Zina hid all her money, keeping a bundle stuck in an old notebook in her office. She heaved a sigh of relief as her sons and her husband boarded the clanking bus for Madrid. Peace and quiet were quickly gone, though. Her neighbor Stoyan dropped in the evening and repeated that Zina's husband owed him two hundred euros.

"Come in a week and I'll pay you," Zina snapped.

Once the knocking on the door halted, it had been magnificent during the first week alone at home. Silence and the TV set took turns to entertain her, and she could not get enough of it. Then the cold evenings and the winter winds annoyed her. She thought of her husband's debts and the sight of the telephone on the table gave her the creeps.

Perhaps, she should ask somebody in for a chat, she thought. After a week of cleaning her flat, she had enough of her TV. She bought a bottle of wine and drank half of it. Zina was a strong woman, unlike the gasbag of a husband, she saw no point in grumbling. She thought of Stoyan, her neighbor, and feared the two hundred bucks her husband owed him.

Zina disliked the man. He and her husband used to be out boozing for hours every day. The man reminded her of the ramshackle Ford in her garage; she could never sell the boneshaker, rust and flat tires all over the place. In the evenings, Zina saw Stoyan leave the pub and stagger on the way to his apartment, stray dogs trailing behind his back.

She had to talk to him, the sooner the better. She had calculated everything and there was no point in postponing the inevitable.

Stoyan looked surprised when he saw Zina at the door of his flat. She stood there, staring at his greasy hair and soiled frayed shirt.

"What do you want?" Stoyan asked. He didn't even try to hitch up his pants. The saggy skin of his belly glistened like a muddy puddle in the dim light. She hated the musty smell in the narrow corridor.

"My husband asked me to take care of you while he's in Spain," she lied.

"What?"

If he had shut up after that sharp *what* she could have lived with it, but the man swore at her. Zina hated obscene words.

"I've cooked some potato soup," she said.

"I don't want your potato soup," Stoyan was about to slam the door in her face. Then he remembered. "You owe me two hundred bucks," he grunted.

Zina thought all men were the same, so she could handle him.

"I've got good plumb brandy," she said.

She had no good brandy at all; there was half a bottle of grapes swill her husband hadn't drunk. She had hidden the booze in a box with a pair of old shoes. Zina would have hidden the whole house from her husband if she'd had the chance.

"You are lying about the brandy," Stoyan said as he pushed her towards the front door, a hesitant stream of hope creeping into his voice all the same.

"It won't hurt you to come and check how it tastes," Zina said. "And my husband owes you two hundred bucks."

She was sure Stoyan would follow her if she descended the stairs to her apartment before he could think things over. Yes. He trailed along after her, dragging his feet, his slippers slow and unenthusiastic. She didn't like men in slippers. Zina wondered where she was going to talk to him. Not in her sitting room, no way. His smell could kill her flowers. The kitchen, yes, she'd take him to the kitchen.

Zina took out two old tumblers she had tucked away in the closet. Stoyan didn't deserve a decent glass.

"Why are the glasses so small? I'm not ill," the man said as he flopped down onto her couch. She had washed the bedcover two days ago, and the greasy stains on his pants made her sick.

"Give me that one," he added, his thick forefinger pointing at the only glass on the table, the one from which Zina drank milk in the morning.

Unwillingly, she gave him the glass and produced the bottle of brandy, a huge flagon, rather dusty and filthy. It was her husband's. Stoyan reached out across the table for it.

"Wait!" Zina said her tone of voice a cup of poison. Stoyan rose from the couch, his pants slipping down the brown pool of his naked skin. She got scared he might get angry so she hurriedly poured some brandy into his glass. Stoyan snatched at it.

"Give me an appetizer," he said. "You lied to me about the brandy. It's rotten."

"I don't have any appetizer," Zina lied. She had quickly calculated that if he went on boozing like that she'd soon have to face an empty flagon. She was mad at herself. You should have hidden some of the booze, you goose, she thought.

"Give me something to eat," Stoyan said, stretching his legs.

Before she could cut a slice of bread for him, Stoyan grabbed at the loaf, tore a big chunk of it and gobbled it down. She stiffened, unable to conceal her disgust, then tore a little piece of bread and chewed at it slowly, deliberating. Zina had some cheese in her fridge, of course, but no, no cheese for that slob. Anyway, a clever woman could produce some appetizer after all. She opened the fridge and took out a jar of small peppers, green like snakes, so hot they could kill the whole town. She took a pepper out of the jar and pretended she was nibbling at it. Stoyan caught hold of the knife, tried to stick it into a pepper, failed, and thrust thumb and forefinger into the jar. She poured another glass of brandy for him—a stingy, grudging one. The man snatched the flagon, filled his glass to the brim, then gulped it down. After a while, he bit off another chunk from the loaf, tried to chew it, and choked. Zina made up her mind: she wouldn't let him swill down all her brandy. She reached out her hand and touched the spot where a patch of his brown skin gleamed, the hard skin pierced by a mass of wiry black hairs.

"What the hell are you doing?" the man snarled, but she paid no attention to his gruff voice. The elastic of his underpants hung loosely in places, torn from the cloth. Zina would not let her husband put on such lousy underpants. Then an icy thought crossed her mind, she had already lost half a flagon of brandy. That sobered her.

"I fell for you years ago," she told the man. That was a barefaced lie, and it made her feel bold. She took the glass from Stoyan and poured the rest of the dreggy liquid into her mouth. It tasted horrible. His skin, like sand paper under her fingers, felt itchy. She filled another glass for him but didn't let him have all the booze to himself. She was smarter than that. "I fell for you, and I'm glad my husband's gone," she said. He gaped at her, spilling some of his brandy on the floor.

"I ... I am friends with ... with your husband," Stoyan mumbled.

"My husband owes you money," Zina said.

He shut up, and the silence encouraged her.

"Sit down," she added, trying not to think of his rusty belt buckle she disliked the minute she saw it.

Zina had the feeling there was so much dust in the folds of his skin that if she threw some seeds of a weed, the weed would strike roots right then and there. The man muttered a word, but Zina paid no attention.

"You'll be all right," she said, calculating it was about time she poured more brandy for him. She tried not to look at his skin. Love had always happened easily with her. It was enough not to look at the man's face while the weeds struck roots in it. She slithered up and down, up and down him, and it felt all right. It almost always did.

"You are g-g-great," Stoyan moaned.

She couldn't care less how great she was.

"Don't breathe in my face," she said.

The big man, his skin hard as sheet iron, tried to sit up. She looked him in the face.

"My husband is your friend, isn't he?"

"Yes," he said.

"He's your friend and I take care of you," Zina said.

"But—"

She hated men who said, "but".

"I hate men who say that word," she said.

"Look here," Stoyan said. "Maybe you don't have to pay me back one hundred bucks," he said.

She thought she'd need a pen soon. When her husband was at home, she made a list of groceries he had to buy from the supermarket. Now, she wanted to be sure she had a similar list for Stoyan. Perhaps at a certain point, she could make him go to the supermarket for her.

"If you give me the same thing one more time," Stoyan began, "You won't have to pay me back the two hundred bucks."

It was cold in the kitchen, and her eyes examined the greasy patches on his pants.

"I've already paid you all my husband owes you," she said. "Get up. Now."

"It was great, Zina," he mumbled.

She looked at his face, white and puffy, and she examined the floor of her kitchen that had been clean before Stoyan mucked it up.

"I paid you back all my husband owed you," she repeated. "Short reckonings make long friends. Go away. Now!"

"But …"

Zina hated men who said, "but". She disliked his skin and his smell. A bitter thought crossed her mind. There were so many other friends her husband owed money to.

V.P.W.

"Isn't she a V.P.W?" I heard Nicko say behind my back. He was talking to another guy from our department whose name I wished I had forgotten. They both laughed as I walked along the corridor. Suddenly I felt my blood rush to my head.

"You'll pay through the nose," I hissed.

"What about me?" the other man asked the arrogant one whose name I hated. "Shall I pay through the nose, too?"

They guffawed; I felt like tearing them into pieces. The three of us worked as interpreters from rare languages into English. No one cared about languages rare or not, and some members of the staff would be fired in a matter of weeks. I was at the end of my tether. My nerves were rags and tatters. A thought had crossed my mind: I'd better concentrate on translating from the French. Alas, no one cared for my perfect French, so I wondered if it would be wise to accept my neighbor's offer to become a governess of her notoriously spoiled son. The child seemed to dislike the way I talked to him and occasionally called after me, "Cuckoo Clara," apparently meaning I was not all there.

"Are you Okay?" Nicko asked.

"She's Okay," the man with the detestable name said. "She's going again to one of her imaginary cities."

"Imaginary Cities" was the short story collection I had written; my colleagues knew no publisher expressed any vibrant interest in my creative outburst. The most enduring consequence of my writing endeavors was that instead of declaring I had a screw loose, Nicko sarcastically remarked I'd founded the next imaginary city at the back of beyond.

"Look here," I said looking Nicko in the eye. "Be careful. That's all I'll say for now."

"A V.P.W. means a Very Pretty Woman," Nicko said innocently.

"She isn't a V.P.W.," the other man objected. "She used to call me John, then suddenly opted for the *Venomous One*, which suits me fine."

We worked in narrow offices in Van Ossel Street, in a good neighborhood that I'd come to love. It had wide streets, steel and glass buildings, parks and more that pleased me. There were no translations coming in and our boss hinted he'd decide who'd be the first one of us three to go. I suspected the two men, Nicko and the venomous one, plotted against me and more likely than not snitched on me to the boss.

The corridor between our offices was a narrow one—dozens of dictionaries lined the walls, and there were a couple of fax machines I rarely used. I was thinking of calling it a day when our boss opened the door to my office and said, "I've made up my mind. I think Clara must go first. She is a V.P.W. and I hope she'll easily find her way home."

The two men heaved deep sighs of relief as the boss added, "Clara, I hope the boys explained to you what a V.P.W. means."

"We did," the Venomous One declared.

"Goodbye and good luck, Clara," the boss said.

"Good luck," Nicko chimed in. The Venomous One, I had already wholeheartedly dubbed *Snake*, also wished me good luck.

I was out of a job, and I didn't know what to do, so I stared at a wall of the narrow corridor hoping my neighbor hadn't changed her mind about taking me up as a governess of her son.

It was quite late in the afternoon, and it was raining.

"These were your dictionaries," Nicko said as he dumped a pile of worn out, battered books at my feet.
I looked out of the window. The cars roared in the cold streets. I imagined my ex-boyfriend's sardonic smile, "You see, you cannot cope with life. You are a no one without me." Then he would add, "I prefer a decent woman to a pretty one, therefore, goodbye."

I collected the dictionaries which I hoped I could sell if worse came to worse.

"Listen, Clara," Nicko said. "I can buy your dictionaries at a very god price."

"And I can buy your old slippers at a very good price," the particularly vicious colleague of mine, the Snake, offered. "I'll be honored, you know."

I went out of the room feeling crushed. One shouldn't despair, I said to myself. The night was beautiful so why not telephone my neighbor and ask if I could become her son's governess.

"Ah, Clara," the woman said. "I've already selected another lady and Tommy simply adores her."

"Oh," I said. "I understand."

"You are a very pretty woman," my neighbor went on. "To be honest with you, Ron, my husband, said he liked you, and I didn't like that."

The old dictionaries weighed a ton each, but one shouldn't despair, I repeated stubbornly. Nicko came rushing to me.

"I was mean," he said.

"You were," I agreed.

"You are a V.P.W," he added. "You were the best looking V.P.W. I've seen."

"So?" I looked him in the eye.

"I like you," he said. "You might have noticed."

Yes, I had. He'd bought me coffee and he'd given me a lift a couple of times.

"You bought me coffee twice," I said.

"You can move in with me," Nicko offered. "I feel sorry for you. You look lost with these heavy tomes tucked under your arm."

"Nicko," I said. "The dictionaries aren't heavy at all."

"You are a lousy translator," he said.

Suddenly the night seemed even colder, the cars gleamed like ice and the wind was sharp and hateful. I knew I was a lousy translator and I knew I didn't have money to pay my rent, so Nicko was an opportunity, and one should never turn a deaf year to an opportunity — that was what my late grandmother used to say. But I imagined Nicko muttering he was only joking when I knocked at his front door as I dragged a suitcase bulky enough to sink a ship. He was an unpredictable weirdo.

"You were not serious about my moving in with you," I said. "You'll throw me out the minute I say something you don't like."

"I'm an opportunity," he said. "One should never turn a deaf ear to an opportunity as your late grandmother used to say. Besides, you don't have money to pay your rent."

The evening seemed awful with the wind hitting my face. Well, I'd lived through worse evenings in my life.

"Don't you think I am a selfish grumbler?" Nicko wanted to know.

"I do," I admitted. "But this is okay with me."

Nicko laughed. "See you tomorrow at Snowdrop Cafe, 7 p.m.," he said.

His words took me to a place I'd been before. They had pulled down the Snowdrop cafe. The man was pulling my leg.

"I still love you," he grinned.

I was just about to unlock the front door of my building when the Snake, the man whose name I hated, came up to me, carrying a bunch of dahlias, inexpensive and drooping ones.

"Hi, Clara," he said. "Can I come in and drink a cup of coffee with you?"

I was about to say he couldn't. The last time Snake drank a cup of coffee with me we didn't go to work for four consecutive days. I'd have to admit he cooked well, he boiled a thing he called Chasseur Vert, which meant Green Hunter, putting into the casserole everything he found in my fridge. He cooked leek soup, too. I loved it. At the end of the fourth day, he said he'd marry me despite the fact I was a lousy translator. I went as far as buying a wedding dress. I asked some friends to my wedding party, but Snake didn't show up at the wedding ceremony he had organized himself. He was the best translator at the agency. I dubbed him *the Snake imbecile,* hoping this would help me kill the pain in the neck the man gave me. It did.

"You probably remembered what happened when we drank coffee together," Snake said. "Everything will be different now. I have drunk mugs and mugs of coffee with other women. It felt different with you."

"Yes," I agreed. "The wedding dress I bought was expensive. I'm still paying it off."

"All the other women, you know...," he paused. "They all bought wedding dresses, too. Only you didn't say I was a lousy lover. The others did."

"They lied," I said and he smiled. "But you are a lousy man," I added.

"I'm an opportunity, and you know what your grandmother said on opportunities. I think you can still use that wedding dress if you try hard enough to remember my name."

I unlocked the front door. My building was a presentable one, hence the exorbitant rent I had to pay for the one room affair. My ex-boyfriend had found a cheap flat for me at a stone's throw from his place. He'd jilted me a couple of times already, but he always came back and said he still got the blues for me.

The Snake Imbecile, whose real name I hated said, "You are thinking of somebody else."

"Yes," I admitted. "I was thinking about my ex-boyfriend."

"Is it the one who gave you the slip after he found me in your bed?" the Snake asked.

"Yes," I said.

"Can I come in for a cup of coffee?" He asked. "I know where I stand with you. You liked my Chasseur Vert, the Green Hunter, don't you remember?"

"No," I said.

The Snake was checking if there were enough things in my fridge to cook another *Chasseur Vert* when the telephone rang.

It was my boss who had just fired me.

"Hi, Clara," he said.

My boss, a famous poet, had written 13 elegies, all of them dedicated to different parts of my body. He'd scribbled each elegiac piece on a scrap of paper then asked me to glue it to my skin where it belonged. He said this made his poetry powerful.

"You are a lousy translator, Clara," the telephone with my boss's voice in it said. "But now I've got nobody to dedicate my poetry to."

I didn't say anything, I thought about the *Chasseur* simmering in the kitchen, and I thought of the coffee I was going to drink five consecutive days with *le Serpent Imbecile*.

"Clara," my boss spoke urgently. "Clara, do you think I'm crazy?"

"Yes," I said. "But I don't mind that."

"Clara, you are a kind-hearted and gentle V.P.W."

I didn't say anything.

"Clara, are you with me? Hey, are with me? Listen, I'm lonely. I wrote a poem. Please, glue it to … you know where. Please, Clara."

I could hear the wind howl in the branches of the trees. It was snowing hard. It was late autumn and I didn't know what to do.

About the Author

Zdravka Evtimova was born in Bulgaria where she lives and works as a literary translator. Her stories have appeared in 31 countries in the world, including USA, UK, Canada, China, Australia, Germany, France, Japan, Italy, etc. The list of her short story collections comprises: *Bitter Sky*, SKREV Press, UK, 2003, *Somebody Else* MAG Press, USA, 2005, *Miss Daniella*, SKREV Press, UK 2007, *Pale and Other Postmodern Bulgarian Stories*, Vox Humana, Canada, 2010, *Carts and Other Stories* Fomite Press, USA 2012; *Time to Mow and Other Stories*, All Things That Matter Press, USA, 2012, *Impossibly Blue and Other Stories*, Skrev Press, UK, 2013, *Endless July and Other Stories*, Paraxenes Meres, Greece, 2013. Her novel **God of Traitors** was published by Book for a Buck Publishers, USA 2007. Her novel *Sinfonia Bulgarica* was published in the **USA** by Fomite Books, 2014; in **Italy** by Salento Books, 2015; in **China** by Art and Literature Press, Shanghai, 2015; in **Macedonia** by Antolog Books, 2015, and in **Serbia** by Draslar Book Partners Books, 2016.

It's Your Turn was one of the ten best award-winning stories in the world short story competition on the topic UTOPIA-2005, Nantes, **France**. Zdravka Evtimova's short story *Vassil* was one of the ten short stories selected as winners in the **world short story competition of Radio BBC, London, 2005.**